Bewitched, Bothered and Dead
A Rat Pack Mystery

Books by Robert J. Randisi
(J.R. Roberts)

Rat Pack mysteries

Talbot Roper novels

The Gunsmith series

Lady Gunsmith series

Angel Eyes series

Tracker series

Mountain Jack Pike series

For more information visit:
www.SpeakingVolumes.us

Bewitched, Bothered and Dead
A Rat Pack Mystery

Robert J. Randisi

SPEAKING VOLUMES
NAPLES, FLORIDA
2022

Bewitched, Bothered and Dead

ISBN 978-1-64540-729-4

TO MARTHAYN
Who, after 29 years,
bewitches me now more than ever.

I'm wild again, beguiled again
A simpering, whimpering child again
Bewitched, bothered and bewildered am I

Richard Rodgers & Lorenz Hart

1940

Prologue: December, 2011

When you're an octogenarian, Thanksgiving, Christmas, and New Year's don't hold the appeal they once did. In fact, it's more a time to look back at holidays past than enjoying the present or what was left of your future.

In fact, Christmas was bittersweet for me each year because Dino had died on Christmas Day in 1995. Holidays always brought that back to me.

It was now the morning after Thanksgiving, an amazing 51 years after the guys had come to Las Vegas to stay at the Sands, on stage and make the movie Ocean's 11. That was when I first met Frank, Dino and Sammy. I had met Joey Bishop before that and seen him a time or two in Vegas. It was Joey who actually introduced me to the rest, starting legitimate friendships with Frank and Dean, something a bit less than that with Sammy, and engendering a dislike for Peter Lawford I was never able to shake.

But somebody I did like had invited me out for Thanksgiving dinner, and I had accepted. So I got my old bones into one of the three good suits I had left and sat on the sofa, waiting for them to come and pick me up, which was part of the deal.

Five minutes before the appointed time, somebody rang my bell from the lobby. I stood up and went to the intercom.

"Hello?"

"Eddie, get your ass down here, old man. We gotta go!"

"I'll be right down."

The voice sounded like somebody who drank and smoked for most of their lives. But when I got down there, I knew I'd be looking at a lady who was thirty years younger than I was, who had never smoked or drank in her life. She just had a voice that was reminiscent of Lizabeth Scott and Lauren Bacall. And for some reason, she liked me.

I left my apartment and took the elevator down.

"Lady waitin', Eddie," the doorman said, as I got off. "Very nice."

"Thanks."

"Don't do nothin' I wouldn't," he called after me.

As I stepped outside, Jacqueline Fairview smiled at me and kissed my cheek. She filled my nostrils with a scent that even aroused an eighty-year-old man—and don't get me started about all the red hair and cleavage.

"The car's over here," she said, sliding her arm into mine.

"You look way too good to be with an old fart like me," I said.

"Shut up and get in the car."

Jackie was rich, which was why she drove a cherry red Porsche. I slid into the front seat, and she went around and got behind the wheel. As she did, her gown flashed her Pilates legs.

It wasn't as if I didn't know why Jackie liked hanging around with me. It was that whole Rat Pack thing. She was a big fan. We met at a recent Rat Pack tribute show that I had been invited to. Folks in Vegas thought that I was one of the last vestiges of that time. For that reason, I got invited to a lot of tribute shows, as well as legitimate activities like a Rickles or Michael Buble concert.

Jackie's money came from family riches, left to her and her brothers by their father when he died twenty years ago. Since then, she partied, because she was rich enough to do it forever. In addition, she had never married, had no kids, so there was nobody to leave the money to. Her intention was to spend it all before she died.

That was a good kind of friend to have.

***

Dinner was at The Bootlegger Italian Bistro, which was an old Rat Pack haunt. Jackie had invited a dozen Rat Pack fans, all of whom knew that I had been friends with the guys.

"I thought you said a few friends," I complained to her as I saw the long banquet table of people.

"Oh, come on, Eddie," she said. "You never let me take you out."

"You drag me out all the time," I corrected her. "Last week it was an Elvis tribute show, the week before that a Deana Martin concert." Dino's daughter was making the rounds singing her dad's songs and had recently released an album of her favorite Christmas songs.

"Well, this isn't a show, it's just dinner," she said, "Thanksgiving dinner at one of your favorite restaurants."

As we sat, the waiters came and started covering the table with food, family style. Growing up in an Italian household, Thanksgiving always combined turkey and lasagna, and that's what was on the table now.

At least Jackie was considerate enough to sit next to me, so I wouldn't have a talkative Rat Pack fan on each side, asking questions.

One thing hadn't changed about the Bootlegger: the food was great. I had a slice of turkey white meat, but most of my plate was taken up by a large slice of lasagna.

"Mr. Gianelli," a young man seated across from me said, "can you tell us what happened the year Howard Hughes came to the Desert Inn for Thanksgiving and refused to leave?"

Howard Hughes was not one of my favorite people. He had come to Vegas a year or two earlier than that, and I had been able to convince him to go back home without buying any property. But in nineteen sixty-six Howard did check into the Desert Inn for Thanksgiving.

"What's your name?" I asked the young man who looked all of twenty.

"Jeffrey, sir."

"Jeffrey, you're a little young to be a Rat Pack fan, aren't you?"

"My father got me started early, sir. I love those guys, especially Dino and Sammy."

"Well, Jeffrey," I said, "stop callin' me sir and just call me Eddie."

"Yes, si—sure, Eddie."

"As far as Howard Hughes goes," I said, "you've managed to bring up a sore subject for me—"

"Eddie—" Jackie said, putting her hand on my arm.

"—but one I don't mind talkin' about," I finished.

Or, rather, I started . . .

Chapter One

Las Vegas,
Two days after Thanksgiving, 1966

I was babysitting one of my high rollers and couldn't respond immediately to Jack Entratter's summons to his office. When I did walk in, he glowered at me.

"Where the fuck have you been?" he demanded.

"Doin' what you pay me to do," I said. "My job. What's up?"

"We've got a problem—" His phone rang at that moment, cutting him off. "What?" he answered, then held it out to me. "It's for you."

"Hello?"

"Eddie. It's Connie."

Connie was one of our better dealers. She worked the blackjack tables, as well as private games—which was what she was supposed to be doing at that moment.

"What is it, Connie?" I asked.

"It's the game, Eddie," she said. "I can't get in."

"Why?"

"The door's locked and nobody'll open it."

"Who are you supposed to be relievin'?" I asked.

"Julie."

Julie was another of our dealers, but she couldn't hold a card or a candle to Connie.

"Where are you now?" I asked.

"At the front desk."

"Okay, meet me up at the door to the room, and tell the front desk to send a maid with you."

"Gotcha."

I handed Jack his phone.

"What's wrong?"

"That was Connie. She's supposed to be working a private game suite, but she can't get in."

"Why not?"

"She says the door's locked, and nobody'll open it."

"Who's she relievin'?"

"Julie."

"What the hell is Julie doin' workin' a high roller private game?" he demanded. "Connie should be in there the whole time."

"Julie's a stunner," I said. "She may not deal as well as Connie, but they ask for her because she's beautiful."

"Well, get the hell up there and find out what's wrong, and then get your ass back here. We gotta talk."

"I gotcha, boss," I said, and hurried out of his office.

***

When I got to the twelfth floor, Connie was waiting at the door with a maid. I read her name tag.

"Diane, you got a pass key?" I asked the maid.

"Yes, sir."

"Open it."

"Yes, sir."

She unlocked the door with her key, and I said, "Okay, thanks. That's all."

"Yes, sir."

"Come on," I said to Connie and led the way into the suite.

6

The large front room was dominated by a round poker table, around which half a dozen men were seated. At that moment Julie was shuffling the deck. I was about to ask what the hell was going on, when I noticed that the men all looked nervous. I took a few steps toward the table and saw why. On the table, at Julie's right elbow, was a .38 revolver. Connie saw it too and grabbed my arm. I waved her back.

"Okay, men, seven card stud, because I really hate dealing Texas Hold 'em. Anybody object? No?"

"Hey, Julie," I said, as calmly as I could. I didn't want to startle her, but her response was, if anything, pleasant.

"Hey, Eddie G.," she said with a smile. "Look, boys, my boss Eddie G.'s here. What's up, Eddie? Wanna watch me work?"

"Well, actually, it's Connie's turn to deal, Julie," I said. "How about we give her the table, and you go get a drink?"

"Lemme think," she said, pausing in her shuffling for a moment. "Naw, I think I'll stay. The fellas, here, they want me to keep dealin' . . . right boys?"

The players all looked up at me with pleading eyes, but said, "Uh, sure, yeah, definitely, keep dealin', babe."

"See, Eddie? You can give Connie some time off."

Julie was blonde, looked as beautiful as ever, but while her voice was very calm her speech pattern was sort of clipped. And when she looked at me, I saw some kind of fever in her eyes.

She went back to her dealing, and Connie stepped close to me and put her lips near my ear.

"Should I send for security? Or cops?"

"No," I said, "I don't want any more guns in the room. Somebody could get killed."

"What about Julie?" she asked. "Is she gonna kill somebody?"

"I don't think so," I said. "Just let me talk to her."

"Be my guest," Connie said, and stepped back.

At the table Julie was saying, ". . . King, six, eighter from Decatur . . ."

Our dealers were told not to say things like, "eighter from Decatur."

"Julie," I said, "I think that's enough."

She turned her head to look at me and put one hand on the gun.

"Eddie," she said, "I'm working."

"No," I said, "you're not. You're fired."

"What?"

"You heard me."

She looked around the table, her hand still on the gun. All the players stared back at her. Then she looked at me, again.

"Why?" she asked.

"Eighter from Decatur?" I said. "Come on, Julie, that's just not professional."

She studied me, no expression on her face, and then suddenly it changed. She smiled, shrugged, and stood up.

"Okay," she said, "it's your casino."

She started to walk past me, and Connie flattened her back against the wall.

"Julie," I said.

"What?"

"I think that gun is casino property."

"This?" She held it up, not pointing it anywhere in particular. "I don't think so. I brought this from home."

"You had a gun at home?"

"Hey," she said, "a girl's gotta protect herself."

"Why bring it to work?" I asked. "To this game?"

"You know, when I deal, everybody else calls the game," she said. "I got tired of that. I wanted to be in charge for a change."

"I see," I said. "But we can't have you carrying a gun on casino and hotel property, Julie. So let me have it, and I'll return it when you go home."

She stared at me, straight-faced again, then shrugged and said, "Okay," handing me the gun.

The men at the table let out a loud, collective sigh of relief.

Chapter Two

"She had what?" Jack Entratter demanded.

"A gun."

"At the table? With our high rollers?"

"Yes."

"Jesus!" he swore. "Where are they now?"

"Well, I offered to leave Connie there to deal, but they all agreed to take a break and go back to their suites."

"Oh, crap," he said. "Let's just hope they're not packin' their bags."

"I offered them free food for the rest of their stay," I said. "Hopefully, they'll stick around."

"And where's the girl?" he asked. "Julie?"

"I let her go home."

"What? You didn't turn her over to the cops?"

"Well, no," I said. "I mean, she didn't really do anything."

"She held a gun on our whales."

"Actually," I said, "she simply took the gun out and set it on the table. She never pointed it at anyone."

"And why does she have a gun?"

"She says for protection."

"From what?"

"From whatever a girl livin' alone needs protection from," I said.

Since we had dealt with a white slavery ring earlier in the year, neither of us wondered what that could be.

"Where's the gun now?" he asked.

"Well," I said, "I gave it back to her."

"You . . . what?" His eyes went wide.

"I mean, it was her property," I said. "I walked her to the front door, unloaded the gun and gave it back."

"And?"

"Oh yeah," I said. "And I fired her."

"Good!" he said, "At least you did something right."

"Hey," I said, "I talked her into giving me the gun and leaving that room. I saved everybody's ass."

"Uh-huh, except you told me she wasn't threatening anybody. The gun was just on the table."

"Yeah, but who knows what would've happened if I wasn't there, huh?"

He picked up his phone.

"Who're you callin'?" I asked.

"The police," he said. "That girl needs help."

"What if she has a permit for that gun?" I asked.

"That's gonna be between her and the cops," he said.

"Jack," I said, "she probably just needs a doctor."

"The cops'll get her one."

"Do we really have to turn her over to the police?" I asked.

"Hey," he said, "she's a beautiful kid. They'll treat her real nice and get her the help she needs."

"Well, just don't call Detective Hargrove," I said. "He's too much of an ass to handle her right."

"Don't worry," he said. "I've got my own contacts. Stay!" he snapped, as I started to get up. "We're not done."

I sat back down while he spoke to his police contact.

". . . and tell them not to hurt her," he finished. "She just needs some help. Yeah, okay, thanks."

He hung up.

"Now," he said, "where were we?"

I had no idea where he was because we had never started, so I waited.

"Howard Hughes."

"What about him?" I asked.

"He's in town at the D.I.," Jack said.

Hughes had come to Vegas a couple of years back, and I took credit for convincing him not to start buying property. But I'd had the feeling—even back then-that he'd return some day.

"What's he doin' here?" I asked.

"He apparently came for Thanksgiving."

"That was two days ago," I said. "Is he still here?"

"Moe says he had a ten-day reservation, but now he won't leave. They tried to get him out because they're expecting high rollers for Christmas and New Years, but he won't budge."

Moe Dalitz was currently the controlling owner of The Desert Inn, as well as the head of the Mayfield Road Mob in Cleveland.

"Moe asked me to ask you to talk to Hughes."

"Me?" I asked. "Why me?"

"He remembers the last time Hughes was here. Says you sent him home with his tail between his legs."

"That's not exactly—"

"I know, but I told 'im you'd do it. You don't wanna make a liar out of me, do ya, Eddie?"

"Hell, no, Jack," I said, "I'll get right over there. I'll probably have to go through Bob Maheu to get to Hughes."

"Hey, you did that last time, too," Jack pointed out.

Maheu spent years working for the F.B.I., until he left to start his own detective agency. After Hughes hired him to investigate a man who was apparently pursuing his fiancé, actress Jean Peters—who

Hughes eventually married, and was still married to—he kept him on. Now he was a high-ranking officer in the Hughes empire.

"You want me to call over there?" Jack asked. "Or we could have Moe arrange a meeting."

"No, no," I said, with a sigh, "I'll handle everything myself. If Hughes doesn't respect that, I figure Maheu will."

"Okay, just let me know what happens."

I stood up and headed for the door.

"And Eddie."

"Yeah?" I said, looking over my shoulder.

"Thanks."

I turned and faced him.

"I didn't know I had a choice."

"You always have a choice, don'tcha?" he asked, smiling. "Do the favor or get fired."

"Right," I said, and left.

Chapter Three

I decided not to make any calls from Entratter's office, so I took the elevator back down to the lobby and walked over to the casino floor.

"Eddie! Eddie!"

I turned and saw the new pit boss we'd just promoted coming toward me.

"What's up, Bernie?"

"Danny Kaye wants to raise the limit at the blackjack table."

"Danny Kaye plays blackjack?"

Bernie frowned.

"I think it's Danny Kaye. Maybe it's Red Skelton. I can never tell these guys apart."

"Okay," I said, "whichever one it is, go ahead and raise the limit. They're good for it."

"Yeah, okay."

"And Bernie!" I snapped as he started away.

"Yeah, Eddie?"

"Start recognizing our guests."

"Right," he said, shrugging. "Maybe it's Alan King."

"Go," I said, waving him away.

As I crossed the casino floor to the Garden Room, which some people had started calling the Garden Café, I thought about the fact that Jack Entratter had never offered me an office. Then again, I had never asked. I guess I just preferred being on the casino floor as much as possible, but when I needed a phone, I had to use either the Garden Room, or the Silver Queen Lounge.

The Garden Room was doing a brisk business, and I decided to have lunch while I went over in my head what I was going to say to Maheu to get him to let me see Hughes.

I had a regular booth in the room that was always available. Some of the diners I passed were players I knew, so we exchanged pleasantries, until I finally reached my booth.

A waitress named Virginia, who I called Gina, came hustling over.

"Busy day, Eddie. You gonna eat?"

"I'll have the breaded veal, Gina, and a phone, when you get a chance."

"Mashed or French fries today?"

"Mashed, with green beans and a salad with ranch dressing," I said, trying to head off any more questions. "And iced tea."

"Comin' up," she said, and flounced off. She returned with the iced tea, and a phone, which she plugged in for me.

"Thanks, doll," I said.

I sipped my tea and picked up the phone. I dialed my buddy Danny Bardini's number. If Robert Maheu was in town, Danny might know what he was up to, since they were both private eyes.

"Maheu?" he said. "Does that mean Hughes is still here? I heard he was at the D.I."

"Yeah, apparently he's refusing to leave," I said. "Have you heard anything about what Maheu might be doin'?"

"I haven't heard a thing, but he's a pro and could be keepin' a low profile. Want me to look closer?"

"Yeah, that'd be good," I said. "Jack wants me to talk to them and see what's goin' on, but I'd like to have somethin' up my sleeve, first."

"I'll do what I can," he promised.

"Thanks, buddy."

"And I'll only charge you lunch," Danny said, "not dinner."

"You're on."

I hung up in time to give my attention to the breaded cutlet Gina brought me.

***

Over lunch I decided to leave trying to see Maheu or Hughes until the next day. I wanted to give Danny time to come up with something.

I spent the shank of the evening trying to convince the high rollers who had been at the table with Julie and her gun to stay with us and not move to another casino. Two of them wouldn't be dissuaded from moving. They told me they came to Vegas to gamble, but not with their lives.

I managed to mollify the others with more free food, as well as complimentary show tickets.

Once that was done, I went to the lounge, sat in the bar and had a bourbon. The conversation around me had to do with the new building that was going up next door, which would have 500 rooms, including a Danny Thomas suite, a Red Skelton suite, and Dean Martin and Jerry Lewis suites. Where the money had come from for this addition was anybody's guess—the mob was at the top of the list—but as I worked on my drink, a bad thought crept into the back of my brain, and I couldn't shake it.

The only person I knew who could corroborate my bad thoughts was Jack Entratter, but would he? I could think of Entratter as a friend all I wanted, but first and foremost he was my boss, and his loyalty was to the owners. He wasn't about to talk to me about the mob behind their backs. But it couldn't hurt to ask, and that was what I planned to do the next morning.

Chapter Four

I spent the night in a room I kept at the Sands for times when I
didn't want to drive home. I was hoping to catch Jack Entratter early
and maybe off guard with my question. As it happened, I was the one
caught off guard when my phone rang. It was Danny.

"I found out somethin' you're not gonna like," he said. "That is,
unless you already know it."

"Hit me with it."

He did.

"No," I said, "I didn't know that, but just yesterday I started wonderin'."

"Makes you wonder what else is goin' on, doesn't it?" Danny
asked.

"It sure does."

"You gonna ask?"

"Oh, I'm gonna ask questions," I said, "to a lot of people."

"Let me know if you need anythin' else from me."

"I will," I said. "Thanks, Danny. I'll call you for lunch."

"I'll be waitin'."

***

"This is early," Jack Entratter said, when I walked into his office.
"What's on your mind? Did you already talk to Maheu?"

"No, not yet," I said. "But I came up with a piece of information—
a piece I wish I'd heard from you, and not from someone else."

I sat down in front of his desk. He apparently decided not to play
innocent.

"So you heard, huh?"

"Howard Hughes is the new owner of the Sands?" I said.

Entratter nodded.

"He paid fourteen point six million dollars," Entratter said. "With the mob out, I may be out, too."

"He's gonna fire you?" I asked.

"I don't know," Entratter said. "I might just quit. I guess it'll all depend on what happens when the addition opens next year."

"So this is why Moe asked for your help?" I asked. "He knows about the sale of the Sands?"

"Everybody's tried to keep it quiet, but once Hughes started building the addition, word got around to the other owners."

"So now . . . what? You think he's gonna try to buy the D.I.? That's why he's squattin' on their top floor?"

"Maybe," Entratter said. "Or maybe he's just tryin' to be a dick."

"So, if you go, where's that leave me?" I asked.

"I think that'd be up to you," Entratter said, "but I swear, if I'm gonna quit, I'll let you know." Entratter got up. "Have a drink with me."

It was early, but as he poured two bourbons, I found myself wanting nothing more than a drink. He handed me a glass, looked me in the eye.

"Vegas is changin'," he said. "It's been comin' for a while."

"What about Frank and his connection to the Sands?" I asked. "Does he know?"

"Oh, he knows," Entratter said, "and he's not happy. He hates Hughes, and the feeling is mutual."

"And why's that?"

"Simple," Entratter said. "Ava."

Howard Hughes had been married to the actress Jean Peters for some time, but everyone knew about his long list of women, which included actresses Terry Moore and Jane Russell. But Ava Gardner was one he couldn't land. She chose Frank and married him.

"Frank's gonna be lookin' for a new theater," Entratter said "Maybe he'll even just stay in Tahoe. Same for Dino and Sammy. They'll all have to find new places."

"And where would you go if you left here?" I asked.

He shrugged his big shoulders.

"Who knows? Maybe Reno."

"This place wouldn't be the same without you and the guys," I said, "and with Howard Hughes in charge."

"If he's smart, he'll keep Carl on."

While Entratter was general manager of the entire property, it was Carl Cohen who was the casino manager. He could and would do his job just as well for Hughes as he had been doing it for the mob.

"I guess we'll just have to wait and see what happens," I said, and we clinked glasses.

Then he walked back behind his desk and sat.

"But why wait?" he said. "Both Maheu and Hughes know you. They'll probably talk to you."

"So you want me to go ahead?" I asked.

"Yeah," Entratter said, "let's just go along like everythin's normal. And if the time comes that it ain't anymore, we'll deal with it then."

"Okay." I finished my drink and set the glass down on his desk. "I'll be in touch."

"And I don't have to tell you—" he started.

"I know," I said. "Keep my trap shut."

Chapter Five

I left Entratter's office with a thought swirling around in my head. If I ended up not working at the Sands anymore, for Jack, where would I end up? I had been there for over ten years. I'd put a lot of time and effort into getting to that point. Starting again somewhere new would be starting over. I was too old for that.

I went to the Garden Room for breakfast and a phone. Jack was right. Getting on with my day and doing something normal would take my mind off the changes that were obviously coming.

I knew the phone numbers of most of the casinos by heart, so I dialed the Desert Inn. When it was Wilbur Clark's Desert Inn, I could just call Wilbur and ask for a favor, but those days were gone. So when the operator answered I asked for Robert Maheu's room, figuring they wouldn't connect me to Hughes.

It was still early enough for Maheu to be in his room, either dressing for the day or having room service. Whatever the reason, he answered on the fourth ring.

"Hello?"

"Maheu?" I said. "Eddie Gianelli."

"Well, well," he said, "I was wondering when we'd hear from you."

"I hate bein' predictable."

"Oh, it's not so much that," Maheu said. "Simply put, it wouldn't be Las Vegas if we didn't hear from Eddie G."

I couldn't tell from his tone if that was sincerity or sarcasm. He was that good.

"I've been hearin' stories," I said.

"Rumors?" Maheu asked.

"I don't think so," I said. "I heard Hughes bought the Sands."

"Oh, that," Maheu said. "That purchase has sort of been under wraps. But I guess not anymore."

"It's not gonna go any further than me," I said, "but I *would* like to see him."

"So would a lot of people," Maheu said. "Me, his wife . . ."

"I'm sure you could call him and set up a meetin'," I said.

"What makes you think he'd agree to see you?" he asked.

"Hey, come on," I said. "He likes me!"

Maheu laughed.

"The funny thing is, you're right, he does, and he doesn't like many people."

"There you go," I said.

"I tell you what," Maheu said. "Why don't we start with you and me having lunch today, and then we can go from there."

"Sounds good," I said. "You want me to come there?"

"Why don't you choose someplace neutral?" he suggested.

I did.

***

I got a booth at the Golden Steer Steakhouse before Maheu arrived. It had a large round table that was usually held for Frank. But the maître d' knew me, and since Frank wasn't in town, there was no problem giving it to me.

The booth was in the front room, so I saw Maheu as soon as he entered, and vice versa.

I stood out of respect, and we shook hands. Maheu was a tall man, well-dressed, closing in on fifty. The waiter came over and while I ordered bourbon, Maheu had scotch.

"Steaks, gents?" the waiter asked.

"Thick and red," Maheu said.

"Same."

"Yes, sirs."

The small, ancient waiter withdrew.

"You're looking well, Eddie," Maheu said. "I understand you've moved out of the pit."

"Yes," I said, "my duties are a little more widespread now."

"So I've heard," he said. "How are your companions, Bardini and that big Brooklyn bruiser?"

"Danny and Jerry are fine," I said. "You're lookin' more prosperous than ever. What'd that suit set you back? Three hundred?"

Maheu smiled.

"I wouldn't wear anything that cheap," he said.

"Of course not," I said, suddenly feeling as if I was wearing pajamas. "So tell me, is Hughes makin' a big move on Vegas?"

"Mr. Hughes does things for one of two reasons," Maheu said. "Profit, or spite. I believe he bought the Sands to spite Sinatra."

"That makes sense," I agreed. "Losing a prize like Ava Gardner to Frank has to sting for a long time. What about the D.I.?"

"I think we're dealing with spite there, as well," Maheu said. "Mr. Hughes simply wasn't ready to check out, and they started to harass him. So now he has no intention of leaving any time soon."

"Is he gonna buy it?"

"Just between you and me," Maheu said, "I wouldn't be surprised. But once he makes a purchase for spite, he makes sure he can turn a profit, as well. Hence, the addition to the Sands."

"So he's gonna be devotin' a lot of time to Vegas, huh?"

"Looks like it," Maheu said. "What do you want to see him about?"

"Well," I answered, "it's like you said to me, how could I let Howard Hughes come to town and not try to see him?"

As the steaks arrived, he said, "I'll see what I can do."

Chapter Six

When Maheu and I went our separate ways, he promised to call by the end of the day to tell me if Hughes would see me.

"Thanks for lunch," he said, because I had picked up the tab.

I passed a few marquees on the way back to the Sands, proclaiming Alan King, Mel Tormé, and Nat King Cole were in town for Thanksgiving. I didn't know who'd be coming in to replace them for Christmas.

I did know that Frank and his family were going to appear with Dean and his family on the Dean Martin Variety Hour for a Christmas show. That was probably why they weren't in the Copa Room that month. When I pulled into the Sands parking lot, the marquee announced Danny Thomas with Al Martino opening for him. Martino had sung the title song for the movie *Hush, Hush Sweet Charlotte* in '64, *and* hit it big in '65 with "Spanish Eyes" but wasn't headlining, yet. It was no slight to open for Danny Thomas, who was the star of the Sands Copa Room. He had opened the room in 1962, and headlined there since. He had become an even bigger star with his T.V. series, *The Danny Thomas Show (formerly make Room for Daddy),* which went off the air in 1964 while still high in the ratings. It was Thomas' decision to end an eleven-year run.

I parked and went inside. One of the desk clerks waved at me, which was usually the case when there was a message.

"What's up, Kevin?" I asked him.

"Mr. Entratter is lookin' for you," the clerk said. "Told us to grab you as soon as you showed up."

"What now?" I said, aloud. "Okay, Kevin, I'll go see 'im. Thanks."

I took the elevator to the fourth floor and was waved in by Entratter's girl.

"He's been asking for you," she said.

"So I heard."

I entered his office. He was sitting behind his desk drinking coffee.

"How'd your lunch with Maheu go?" he asked.

"Fine. I bought him a steak."

"*You* bought *him* a steak?" he asked.

"Well," I said, tossing the receipt onto his desk, "actually you did."

Scowling, he picked up the piece of paper and looked at it.

"He's gonna talk to Hughes and then let me know if he'll see me."

"Is Hughes buyin' the Desert Inn or not?" Entratter asked.

"Maheu was iffy about that," I said. "I'll see what I can find out from Hughes."

"If he sees you."

"He will."

"What makes you so sure?" Entratter asked.

I smiled.

"He likes me," I said. "That's the very reason you told me to try and see him, isn't it?"

"Like hell," Entratter said. "Howard Hughes only likes women, and even them not for long."

"So why were you lookin' for me this mornin'?" I asked.

"Because you don't have enough to do," he said, sarcastically. "I told him you were busy, but he says he wants you to have dinner with him."

"Him who?" I asked. "Who the hell are we talkin' about?"

"Jesus, I didn't say?" Entratter asked. "I must be losin' it. Danny Thomas was askin' if you could eat with him tonight, after his show."

"What the hell does he want with me?" I asked.

24

"You know 'im, don't you?"

"Well, he's played here enough times, and I've seen him once or twice on the casino floor, but I don't know him that well."

"So here's your chance," Entratter said.

"And what if Hughes wants to see me tonight?" I asked.

"Work it out, Eddie," Entratter said. "What can I say? You're in demand."

I sighed heavily.

"Okay, should I call 'im and set it up? Or do you wanna do it?"

"Just be there after the show," Entratter said.

I stood up to leave, then hesitated.

"Jack, Frank's not in town, is he?"

"No," Entratter said, "not yet."

"Has he heard about Hughes buyin' the Sands?"

"Yeah, and he's not happy about it," Entratter said. "If he does come to town, I'm kinda worried about what will happen."

Everybody knew Frank had a temper. There were all kinds of stories about it, and even JFK had experienced it, although I never had. Not personally anyway.

"Maybe I'll give him a call," I said. "I might be able to head off trouble."

"You do that," Entratter said, "and I'll give you a big fat raise."

"I'll take it."

"It might be the last thing I do before the door hits me in the ass on the way out!"

Chapter Seven

I had to stay around the Sands to await Bob Maheu's call. If I didn't hear from him, I'd have dinner with Danny Thomas, and then repeat the process the next day. Just stay around and wait for the call.

I remained on the casino floor so a desk clerk or bell hop would be able to find me. I decided not to go to the Copa Room until after Danny Thomas' show, rather than watching it. I'd seen it before. So I stayed around the casino until late, then went to my room and changed for dinner. I was hoping the phone would ring while I was there, but by the time I tied my tie and was ready to leave, it still hadn't.

I went down to the Copa Room, entering in time to see Danny Thomas' last encore. I got backstage before he came off for the final time.

"Eddie G.," he greeted, spreading his arms. "I'm real glad you agreed to eat with me tonight." His face was glistening with perspiration.

"Thanks for invitin' me," I said.

"Just let me shower and change. There'll be a car waiting for us."

"Take your time," I said. "I can wait."

***

It took Thomas half-an-hour, and then we were in the car he had arranged for, rather than have the Sands make the arrangements.

"I'm used to doing things for myself," he explained, as we got into the black sedan.

Thomas chose The Bootlegger Italian Restaurant, where I had been many times with Frank and Dino, so it wasn't a long ride. When we arrived, the maître d' took us to a table in the back that was apparently Danny Thomas' regular table. I knew where Frank's table was, but didn't know Danny had a smaller, more intimate one.

Neither one of us spent too much time on the menu. I ordered spaghetti and meatballs while he went for the lasagna. He wasn't a heavy drinker, but he had a glass of red wine, saying that one glass mellowed him out after a show. I ordered a bourbon on the rocks. He also lit a cigarette while we waited for our food. That was one filthy habit I had never fallen into.

"What's on your mind, Mr. Thomas?" I asked. "Jack Entratter said you asked for me specifically."

"Look, Eddie," Thomas said, "we don't know each other well, but I wish you'd call me Danny, not Mr. Thomas."

"No problem, Danny."

"I hear good things about you in Vegas, Eddie," he said. "And not only from Frank, Dino and Jack Entratter. It sounds to me like you got this town in your hip pocket."

"Not everybody thinks so," I said.

"Well, for the purposes of this conversation," Danny said, "I'm going along with it."

"Okay," I said. "I got Vegas in my pocket. Now what?"

"Now I need your help."

"With what?"

"Do you know about St. Jude?"

St. Jude was a hospital Danny had founded to treat children at no expense to their parents. That meant that all of the medical bills would be paid by outside donations.

"Of course," I said. "It's a wonderful thing you've created."

"Yes, well," he said, looking both dismayed and annoyed, "that wonderful thing isn't developing the way I had hoped, since it opened in sixty-two."

"How do you mean?" I asked.

"I mean," he said, "the money isn't coming in the way I'd hoped, or it is and it's being mismanaged."

"Ah ha," I said. "Mismanaged how?"

"Gambling, maybe," he said. "I thought I could trust the people I have running St. Jude. Now I'm starting to wonder."

"So this is where I come in?" I asked.

"I need somebody who knows Vegas," he said. "The casinos, the people . . . I need to know if somebody is skimming and gambling the money here. Or maybe Atlantic City. Can you check there, as well?"

"I have some contacts there, but what if they're skimming and doing somethin' else with the money?" I asked. "Like bettin' it at the track? Or the stock market?"

"Once we determine whether or not they're gambling, I can look elsewhere. I'll hire a private eye, or something."

"You may not have to," I said. "I know somebody."

"And they'll work on this with you?"

"Oh yeah," I said. "I wanna be thorough. Have you gone to the police, Danny?"

"Not yet," he said. "Not until I know something for sure. I don't want this getting out, Eddie. It could ruin St. Jude before we really get started. Whataya say, Eddie? Can you give me a hand with this?"

Other than trying to talk with Howard Hughes and my regular job at the Sands, I had nothing else on my plate.

"I don't see why not," I said. "Who do you have in mind for it?"

"There are three people who run St. Jude," Danny said. "Eventually, I was going to get it down to one of them, but I still don't know which one."

"Well, if you find one of them gamblin', that'll help you narrow it down."

He produced an envelope. "Here are their names and particulars," Danny said. "Think you can take it from there?"

"Why not?" I said, accepting the envelope. "I'll nose around, see what I can find out."

"All I need," he said, "is confirmation that one of them is gambling."

"What if they're usin' their own money?" I asked.

"I guess that'll depend on how much you find out they're gambling," he said. "If it's big money—"

"—then it's St. Jude's, huh?"

"That'd figure, wouldn't it?"

"Are these people on salary?"

"Well, yes, they won't do the work for free."

"Big salaries?"

"They're not gonna get rich from it," Danny said.

"Do they have other sources of income?"

"Sure," Danny said. "One of them is a doctor, the other two are organizers. But none of them are rich enough to be gambling big money."

The waiter came with our plates and set them down. I had a second drink, while Danny asked for a beer.

Chapter Eight

I stuck to my promise to Jack Entratter and didn't mention Howard Hughes. Danny asked me some questions about my past, but after a few questions I managed to steer the conversation around to him. It wasn't hard. Show biz types like talking about themselves. He told me some stories about his show, how much he liked the kids he'd been working with, Rusty Hamer and Angela Cartwright.

"I'm thinking about updating the show, maybe doing something like 'Make Room For Grandpa,' or something like that."

"Sounds good," I said.

We took the car back to the Sands and shook hands in the lobby.

"I have a few more days in the Copa Room," Danny said. "After that I'll be going home. I'll leave you my number."

"We'll talk again before you leave," I promised.

"Thank you, Eddie," Danny said.

On his way to the elevator, he was stopped by several people, who complimented his T.V. series, or his Copa show. He was polite to all of them.

Once he boarded the elevator, I went to the front desk to check for messages.

"Kevin, anything for me?"

"No, sir," Kevin said. "Nobody's lookin' for you."

"That's good," I said. "I should be around for the rest of the night, if anyone calls or comes lookin'."

"Got it, Mr. Gianelli."

I went onto the casino floor to soak up some normalcy. The bells and coins of the slot machines often drowned out the sound of chips-on-chips on the card tables. And often there was the sound of whoever was performing in the lounge wafting out onto the floor.

I took a walk around, exchanging greetings with people I knew, fielding questions from pit bosses and dealers, until I reached the entrance to the Silver Queen Lounge. At the moment no one was on stage. I knew a late show would be coming on soon, but I could sit and have a drink in the quiet for a little while and go over some of what Danny Thomas and I had talked about.

I ordered a drink and took out the envelope Danny had handed me. There were two men, and a woman. What I needed to do was circulate their names to the casinos, see if anyone knew them as high rollers. There wouldn't be much more for me to do if one of them got recognized.

I looked at the three names. None of them rang a bell, but then we didn't travel in the same circles. I was sure Danny Thomas had his reasons for involving them in his St. Jude project. Or, at least, he thought he did. He might have made a mistake about one of them.

On the other hand, he could be wrong and none of them were involved. It could've been someone else, entirely, and have nothing to do with Vegas. Someone could have been taking money and going to the track.

I folded the paper and put it away, asked the bartender for a phone. I dialed Danny Bardini's home number.

"Lunch tomorrow?" I said, when he picked up.

"I thought you'd never ask," he said.

***

To make it easy, we met for lunch in the Garden Room. That was okay with Danny, since he liked the food there.

"Meat Loaf," he told the waitress, Gina.

"Comin' up, handsome," she said, smiling at him. "And you, Eddie?"

"Somethin' simple," I said. "A turkey sandwich and fries."

"You got it."

She walked away, came back quickly with a coffee pot and two cups, then went off again.

"Maheu's keepin' his head down," Danny said. "I don't have anythin' yet. How about you?"

I told him about my dinner with the man.

"Spite?" Danny repeated, laughing. "He really said that?"

"He did."

"But if he starts buying up casinos, he's not only spitin' Sinatra, he's spitin' the mob."

"Apparently, that doesn't concern him."

"Well," Danny said, "I suppose he's bigger than them."

"I suppose he's bigger than anybody," I said. "The mob, the law . . ."

"I can't imagine what it must be like to have that much money," Danny said, shaking his head, "havin' all those beautiful women—"

"Yeah," I said, cutting him off, "but he's also batshit crazy."

"There is that." He sipped his coffee. "You think Maheu will get you in to see him?"

"I think so," I said, "but I've also got other fish to fry."

"Like what?"

"Not what?" I said. "Who. Danny Thomas."

"I saw his name on the marquee," Danny said. "Big name. How well do you know him?"

"Not well, at all," I said, "but he came to me for help. Bought me dinner last night, after his show."

"What's on his mind?"

"St. Jude."

"Danny Thomas' charity?" Danny said. "Is he havin' trouble?"

"He thinks somebody might be skimmin'," I said. "And gamblin' the money."

"Ah," Danny said, "now comin' to Eddie G. makes sense. What's your first move?"

"He gave me three names," I said. "I'm gonna circulate them, see if anybody recognizes any of them."

"Solid detective work," Danny said. "You want me to do anythin'?"

"Keep your ear to the ground about Hughes and Maheu," I said, sliding a piece of paper across the table. "but take a look at these."

He looked at the paper.

"These the three St. Jude people?"

"Yeah."

"One's a woman."

"I noticed that," I said. "I'm wonderin' if one of them might be skimmin' and usin' the money for somethin' else."

"Like what?"

"Like the track, or the market."

"Ah . . . that's a good thought. Want me to check it out?"

"I figure you got connections everywhere I don't," I said.

"I can check tracks, bookies, and believe it or not, I got a connection on Wall Street."

"So why don't you have a portfolio?"

"Because," Danny said, "I got a connection on Wall Street. That stuff's worse than the track." He tucked the three names into his pocket. "I'll see what I can dig up. Anythin' else?"

"Maybe later I'll introduce you to Danny Thomas."

"That's okay," he said, "you don't hafta do that. Now if you could introduce me to Sherry Jackson, that'd be somethin'. What a doll!"

"I'm sure Penny would love that," I said. Penny was his long-time secretary-turned-girlfriend.

Gina came out carrying our plates, set them down in front of us, refilled our coffee cups and smiled at Danny.

"Anything else, handsome?" she asked.

"I'm good for now, sweetheart," he said, "but if I think of somethin', you'll be the first to know."

We both watched her walk away, then started to eat.

Chapter Nine

After lunch with Mr. Danny Thomas, I stopped in on Jack Entratter to fill him in on the Thomas problem.

"That's what happens when you try to be a do-gooder," Entratter groused.

"Hey," I said, "if he could get that thing goin' the way he wants, it would be somethin'."

"Yeah, yeah, I know," Entratter said. "Don't mind me. I'm in a foul mood, these days."

"I know you don't like change," I said. "I'm not crazy about it either."

"We had this town runnin' just right," Entratter said. "If our guys are out, and businessmen come in and run things . . ." He waved his hand in disgust. "I hate bean counters."

"What was the idea behind sellin' the Sands?" I asked.

"He just offered too much money," Entratter said. "They couldn't refuse."

"An offer they couldn't refuse, huh?" I said, shaking my head.

"I guess," he said. "You heard from Maheu yet?"

"No, but I bet he calls today."

"Well, don't bother tellin' me when you hear, just go and see Hughes. You can tell me about it after."

"You got it," I said, standing up. "Try not to let this all get you down, Jack."

"Easy for you to say," he responded. "You'll probably keep your job—-and if you don't, another casino will hire Eddie G."

"And you don't think another casino would hire Jack Entratter?" I asked. "Come on!"

"I don't know if I want to work in another casino," Entratter said. "This has been my place for a long time, Eddie."

"Think about it, Jack," I suggested. "Somebody'll want a man with your experience."

"Yeah," he said, "okay, thanks."

I left his office but didn't get far. His girl waved me down and held her phone out.

"For you."

I took it from her.

"Hello?"

"Eddie," a man's voice said, "Bob Maheu."

"Nice to hear from you."

"Mr. Hughes says he'll see you."

"When?"

"Tonight," Maheu said. "He wants you to come to his suite at the D.I."

"I can do that," I said. "You gonna be there?"

"I'll meet you in the lobby, say seven?" Maheu answered. "But I won't be going up with you. Mr. Hughes runs his businesses—and his life—over the phone. In fact, you're lucky he's agreed to see you. I figured you'd just get to talk to him on the phone."

"Well, it's like you said, Mr. Maheu," I responded. "He likes me."

"Eddie," Maheu said, "I think you said that. I'll see you a little before seven. Be prompt, or he might change his mind."

"Don't worry," I said, "I'm not gonna miss this."

When I handed the phone back to Jack's girl I decided not to go back into his office. I'd just do what he said and report to him after.

***

I got to the Desert Inn lobby at six-forty-five, and Maheu was there.

"I thought I'd beat you," I said.

"Don't ever try," Maheu warned.

"No, I meant—"

"I know what you meant," Maheu said. "Wait here and I'll call up-stairs."

He walked to a house phone, spoke briefly, and then came back.

"You can go up."

"What floor?"

"The top."

"What room?"

Maheu smiled.

"The entire floor."

"Figures," I said.

I went to the elevators and took one to the top floor. I got off the elevator, looked both ways, saw an open door and walked to it. In the past I had seen several different versions of Howard Hughes. I'd seen him well-dressed and groomed, I'd seen him with wild, stringy hair and long, unkempt fingernails. And I'd seen him sitting naked on a sofa with a napkin across his crotch. I didn't know what to expect when I entered the suite.

I didn't have to wait long.

As soon as I walked in, I saw a man standing with his back to me, wearing a silk bathrobe. When he turned, I saw it was Howard Hughes, sporting a long, scraggly beard, and wearing only boxer shorts beneath the robe, which was hanging open.

"Eddie G," Hughes greeted me. "Good to see you. I knew when I came back to Vegas we'd be meeting up again. You want a drink?"

"I think I need one," I said, marveling at this still new vision of Howard Hughes.

"Help yourself at the bar," Hughes said. "Excuse the robe, but my allodynia is acting up."

I knew he suffered from that ailment, which made the touch of clothing painful.

"Hey, I've got a New York Strip Steak and some peas coming up, along with a salad. You interested?"

"No, thanks," I said. "I'll make do with a bourbon."

"After that I'm getting some French vanilla ice cream. You sure you don't want to eat?"

"Positive," I said, moving around behind his bar. "You want anythin' from here?" I asked.

"Just a glass of milk, thanks," Hughes said.

He sat on the sofa, allowed the robe to flap wide open, and I was grateful for the boxer shorts. The last time I'd seen him in such a position he'd only been covered by a pink napkin.

I made myself a bourbon and came back around the bar.

"Mr. Hughes—" I started.

"Hey, it's Howard," he said, cutting me off. "You know, I consider you one of my few friends, Eddie G."

"Really?" I asked. "Why is that?"

Hughes laughed.

"I'll tell you why," he said. "You talk straight, and you don't want anything from me. And by anything, I mean money."

"Well, then," I said, "maybe the question is, what do you want from me?"

Chapter Ten

"What makes you think I want something from you?" he asked. "I thought you asked to see me."

"Yeah," I said, "but you wouldn't have agreed to see me if you didn't want somethin'."

Hughes smiled.

"See? You're smart, that's why I like you."

"Howard—"

There was a knock on the open door, and then a bellman wheeled in a cart.

"Ah, my steak. Over here, please," Hughes said.

"Yessir," the bellman said and wheeled it over. "Shall I remove the cloche?"

"I'll take care of it," Hughes said.

The bellman stood there.

"Oh, yes," Hughes said. "Um, Eddie, can you tip this guy for me? I don't have any cash in my robe. I'd appreciate it."

"Yeah, sure."

I gave the guy a few bucks and sent him on his way. By the time I turned back to Hughes, he had the cloche off his plate and was already separating the peas by size with his knife and fork. He would only eat the largest ones.

Once he had the peas arranged, he went to work on the steak, cutting it into pieces.

"You sure you don't want something?" he asked. "I can call down and have it brought right up."

"No, thanks," I said. "I'm good."

"Well then, do you mind if I eat while we talk?"

"No, go right ahead."

I went over and sat on a bar stool with my drink.

"Okay, Eddie, this is it," Hughes said. "You know I bought the Sands."

"I just found that out, actually," I said. "It was a well-kept secret."

"I'd like it to stay that way a little longer," he said.

"And do you intend to buy the Desert Inn?"

He smiled.

"I didn't," he said, "until they pissed me off. They want me to leave so they can rent all this floor's rooms out to their New Year's revelers."

"And?"

"And I don't want to leave," he said, chewing his steak. "So I'm considering my options."

"What were your intentions when you came to town?"

"Look over the construction of the addition to the Sands, and to find other properties to buy. I'm thinking about the New Frontier, perhaps the Landmark."

"Why not the Golden Nugget, or the Flamingo?"

"Bugsy's place?" Hughes asked. "Maybe some time in the future. The mob is not easy to negotiate with."

"Are you afraid of them?"

"Afraid? Why? Because they killed Kennedy?"

"Did they?"

"Didn't they?" He cut another piece of steak and ate it. "In any case, I'll start small."

"The Sands isn't starting small."

"That was only because of that Dago, Sinatra. I wanted to make sure he never performed there again."

"There are plenty of places that'll take him on," I said. "Will you buy them all?"

"The Sands was his place," Hughes said. "I'll be satisfied to take that away from him."

"Then why did you want to see me?"

"You called me, remember?" Hughes said. "Did Entratter send you?"

"He thought I might be able to get you to . . . vacate these premises."

"Are you telling me Jack Entratter asked you to come here and talk to me?" Hughes asked. "Or that Moe Dalitz asked Entratter to ask you to do it?"

"What's the difference?"

"There's a difference," Hughes said, "when it comes to leverage. I never go into a business negotiation without leverage."

I had to consider my answer. After all, I wasn't sent there to give him any kind of leverage.

"I don't know whose idea it was," I said, "but I agreed to do it."

"And so you have," Hughes said. "You can go back to Entratter and tell him you did your job. Now," he put his knife and fork down, "I've got something I want you to do for me."

"What's that?"

"Find out who's willing to sell and who isn't," Hughes said.

"Like the Landmark?"

"Or the Golden Nugget, as you suggested," Hughes said. "Or I can start smaller. Perhaps The Silver Slipper. I can see the damn lights from my window at night. It keeps me awake."

"That's reason enough to buy it?" I asked.

"I have enough money to buy what I want for any reason," Hughes said.

The Sands was a perfect example of that. He'd bought it just to spite Frank. That was because Frank not only went to bed with Ava, but

41

married her. I was also one up on Hughes with the first one. Not that I'd ever tell him, or Frank, for that matter. That was between Ava and me.

"What makes you think I know who'll sell?" I asked. "Or that they'll tell me."

Hughes smiled broadly, picked up his knife and stabbed at his steak. "You're Eddie G.!"

Chapter Eleven

When I left Howard Hughes, I had a plan. Meet with all the casino owners I could and see if I was able to convince them *not* to sell out to him. But I allowed him to believe I was on his side.

It was no surprise to find Bob Maheu waiting for me in the lobby.

"You gonna ask me how it went?"

"I know how it went," Maheu said. "Mr. Hughes wouldn't allow it to go any other way. He can be very, very convincing when he wants something."

"You know what, Bob?" I said. "Fuck you."

He was laughing as I walked out.

***

I told Jack Entratter that I had allowed both Hughes and Maheu to believe I was in their camp.

"Did he offer to pay you?" Jack asked.

"No."

"Then why would he think you'll do what he wants you to do?"

"It's like Maheu said," I answered. "They both think there's no other way to go."

"Hughes ain't gonna be happy when he finds out what you're really plannin' on doin'."

"Too bad for Hughes," I said. "The longer I can keep him from takin' over Vegas, the better."

"Watch your back, Eddie," Entratter advised.

"I got a better idea," I said. "I'll have somebody else watch my back."

He frowned because he knew who I meant.

***

Danny Bardini was my best friend. We had been kids together, back when he was my older brother's best friend. When my brother died, we just came together.

But Jerry Epstein had to run a close second.

When I called him and told him what I was doing he said, "Howard Hughes, huh? Sounds like fun, Mr. G. I'm on the next plane."

"Fly first class, if you can," I said. "We'll reimburse you."

"You got it!" he said, happily.

***

Jerry got a flight that evening, and I picked him up at McCarran. As usual, he drove my Caddy back to the Sands while we caught up.

"Whatja do for Thanksgivin', Mr. G.?"

"I had a turkey dinner in the Garden Room."

"Alone?"

"Yeah, alone."

I knew he wanted to ask about my family in Brooklyn, but he knew better.

"What about you?"

"My new girlfriend wanted to make me Thanksgiving dinner," he said.

"And?"

"And we called it quits right after," he said. "She's a horrible cook."

I knew that was reason enough for Jerry to break up with a girl.

"What've you been up to, otherwise?" I asked.

"I been doin' some collectin'," he told me.

"Leg breakin'?" I asked.

"When they don't pay."

"Isn't that a little beneath you, Jerry?"

"Since Mo Mo went to prison, the good work has dried up," he told me.

Giancana had finally been sent to prison in '66, and when he got out a year later, he had been deposed and replaced by "Joey Doves" Aiuppa. So Mo Mo had fled to Mexico and was laying low.

"Joey Doves has his own men," Jerry told me. "What's been goin' on with you, besides wantin' to screw Howard Hughes?"

I told him about Danny Thomas.

"I love that guy!" he gushed. "*Make Room For Daddy* was one of my favorite shows, even after they changed the name to *The Danny Thomas Show*. Think I'll get a chance to meet 'im?"

"If I can work it out, sure," I said. "Why not?"

"You got a broad these days, Mr. G.?" he asked. "I mean, I know you got broads. They're all over the place here. But do you got, ya know, a main lady?"

"Nobody in particular, Jerry," I said. "How about you?"

"Aw, you know me, Mr. G.," he said. "I like ta play the field. But I got a coupla whores I use."

As we approached the Sands, Jerry saw the addition that was going up next to it, I told him about Hughes buying the place.

"What? Sonofabitch! That surprises me."

"Yeah, me, too," I said. "Apparently, he just wanted to screw Frank out of playing here ever again."

"What the fuck—" Jerry said. "There's plenty of other casinos in town that'll want 'im."

"You got that right," I said, "but it looks to me like the guys are gettin' split up."

"No more Rat Pack?" Jerry asked, as we pulled into the parking lot.

"Frank calls it the Summit," I said, "but yeah, that's what it looks like. A few months ago, Sammy was here with Jerry Lewis. Now Frank's gonna go somewhere else and, believe me, Dino's not gonna stay if Frank's gone."

"Vegas is changin'," Jerry said.

"I know," I said, as we got out of the car, "and not for the better."

Chapter Twelve

What would Las Vegas be like without the Rat Pack to entertain it, and without the mob to run it? Oh my God, what if they decided to make it a family friendly place? What if people started to bring their children? I shuddered.

"Mr. G.?" Jerry said.

"What?"

"You look like you seen a ghost."

"Not a ghost," I said. "Just a horrible future."

We were seated in the Garden Room because airline food wasn't enough to sustain Jerry, even though he was now diabetic and had lost some weight, he was still a bruiser.

He ordered grilled chicken and a salad but kept stealing French fries from my burger plate. That was part of his diet, not ordering his own fries.

"So you're gonna warn the casino owners against sellin' to Mr. Hughes," Jerry said, reminding me of where we'd left off.

"That's right."

"He ain't gonna like that."

"If he finds out that's what I'm doin'," I agreed.

"If that happens, he'd have that Maheu guy take care of it," Jerry said, "and by that I mean—"

"I know what you mean," I said, cutting him off, "that's why I've got you to watch my back."

"You can count on me, Mr. G.," he said, snagging two fries at once. "So what're ya gonna do about Mr. Thomas' problem?"

"I'm gonna draft more help."

"The shamus?"

I nodded.

"Danny's the one who told me about Hughes buyin' the Sands," I said. "Now I'm gonna ask him to look into the Danny Thomas problem for me. We've gotta check Vegas and A.C."

"He'll like that, won't he?" Jerry asked. "You gonna introduce 'em?"

"No," I said, "I don't necessarily want Danny Thomas to know about Danny Bardini."

"What about me?" Jerry asked. "Don't forget about me."

"Just give me a chance to figure out when."

"Sure thing, Mr. G.," Jerry said. "Whatever you say."

"Finish my fries, and we'll get you to your room," I said, around my last bite of burger.

"Well," he said, "I shouldn't," and slid my plate over to his side of the table.

***

As usual I got Jerry a suite. He was a big man who needed lots of room.

He came back to the living room after dumping his suitcase in the bedroom.

"Where are we gonna start?" he asked.

"I'm thinkin' one end of the strip to the other," I said, "and then Fremont Street."

"I like Fremont Street," he said.

"You like it because it's sleazy," I said.

"Pretty much," Jerry agreed. "Sometimes the strip is too glitzy for me."

"I thought bein' around me was improving your taste, Jerry," I commented.

"Oh sure, Mr. G.," he said, "you've improved me a lot, but that don't mean I don't like to go divin' sometimes."

Jerry called visiting dive bars "going diving."

"You know what?" I said. "Let's start with Fremont Street and then we can stop in and see Danny."

"That works for me," Jerry said. "We can visit that Horseshoe coffee shop."

"We just ate."

"We'll be hungry later, won't we?"

"No doubt," I said. "Let me call Danny and tell 'im we're comin'."

***

We drove down to Fremont Street and parked behind Binion's Horseshoe. Danny's office was right down the street. While we were there, I'd be able to talk to the owners of the Horseshoe, the Four Kings, the El Cortez and a few others about Hughes. But first we were stopping at Danny's office.

"Hey Eddie," Penny said, as we walked in, and then "Hiya, big guy."

"Hi, Penny." Jerry was always very respectful and shy around Penny, especially since she had gone from Danny's secretary to his girlfriend.

"The boss is waiting on you," she said.

"Thanks."

"Coffee?" she asked.

"No thanks," I said quickly, before Jerry could answer.

We entered Danny's office, and he looked up from his desk.

"Hey, big Jerry!" he said, standing up.

"Big dick," Jerry said, and they shook hands. They had developed a grudging admiration and respect for each other over the past few years.

"Have a seat, guys, and tell me what's up?" Danny said.

I explained about my meetings with Howard Hughes, and with Danny Thomas.

"St. Jude, huh?" Danny said, shaking his head. "I'm always suspicious of charities. That money's goin' in somebody's pocket."

"Well, he agrees with you, Danny," I said. "And he wants to know whose pocket."

"You want me to go to A.C.?" Danny asked.

"If you have to," I said. "I think I'm gonna be busy with this Howard Hughes thing. I shudder to think of what Vegas will be like if he gets in here."

"Hey, things are changin', bubba, and there's not much we can do about it," Danny said.

"Well," I said, "I can try."

"Is Thomas gonna know about me?" Danny asked.

"Not unless he has to."

"I might have to talk to him."

"You tell me when, and I'll arrange it," I said. I took out the envelope Danny Thomas had given me. "This is the info on the three people he suspects."

"Am I gettin' paid for this?" he asked, accepting the envelope.

"Not in love," I said, "or money. This is strictly a favor."

"You and your celebrity favors," Danny moaned.

Chapter Thirteen

Jackie Gaughan bought the El Cortez from William Moore and J. Kell Houssels, who had purchased it from Bugsy Siegel, before Siegel went on to build the Flamingo. Jackie was in his office and agreed to see me right away.

"Eddie G.," he said, sticking his hand out. "Whataya, slummmin'?"

"Hey, Jackie," I said. "This is my pal, Jerry Epstein."

"Hey, any pal of Eddie's," Jackie said, and shook hands with Jerry.

Jackie was a little guy in his forties who, at one time, would own 25% of the real estate in downtown Vegas.

Jackie sat behind his desk and listened to what I had to say.

"Eddie," he said, when I was done, "Howard Hughes can kiss my ass. I ain't never sellin'."

"That's what I figured, Jackie," I said. "That's why I started with you. I knew how you'd feel."

"Well, Benny Binion's gonna tell ya the same thing," Jackie said. "And probably Buck Blaine at the Nugget."

Guy McAfee had built the Golden Nugget and owned the Frontier, but he retired in 1960, turning control over to his investor, Buck Blaine.

"Glad to hear you still feel that way, Jackie," I said, stepping to the desk and shaking hands with him again.

"This is my town, Eddie, and it ain't never gonna be Howard Hughes'," Jackie said. "If ya want, you can tell 'im that for me."

"I think you're going to be hearin' from him, Jackie."

"Then I'll tell 'im myself," Jackie said. "You and the big fella here, stop off at the bar and have a drink on me. I'll call down there and let 'em know."

"Why not?" I said. "Thanks, Jackie."

We went downstairs and stopped off at the V.I.P. Lounge for that drink—a beer for Jerry, and a bourbon for me—before we moved on.

We got much the same result when we visited the Horseshoe, the Four Kings, the Golden Nugget, and on down the line. I could've done all of this on the phone, but I wanted to look people in the eye when I mentioned Hughes. Not once did I get the feeling they had already been contacted and made a deal. The downtown crowd was firmly entrenched in their casinos. Now it was time to go and talk to the Strip owners.

***

We drove back to the Sands. I decided to simply walk the strip and stop into each casino. However, as I entered, the hotel clerk waved frantically to me.

"Mr. G., that kid's arm is gonna come off," Jerry said.

"We better see what he wants," I said, and we walked over to the desk.

"Mr. Gianelli," Kevin said, "I got an urgent message for ya." He held a slip of paper out to me, then whispered, "It's from Frank Sinatra."

I stage whispered back, "Thanks, Kevin."

We walked away from the desk, and I read the message.

"What's with Mr. S.?" Jerry asked.

"He wants me to come up to his suite as soon as I get this," I said, folding the message. "I didn't even know he was in town."

"He ain't performin', is he? I saw Danny Thomas' name outside."

"No," I said. "I'm afraid this might have something to do with Howard Hughes bein' in town. Jerry, why don't you hang around down here while I see what's on Frank's mind."

"Whatever you say, Mr. G.," Jerry said. "Just call down if ya need me."

Frank's temper was legendary, but I was hoping I wouldn't need Jerry's help to handle him.

Chapter Fourteen

When I knocked on his door it was opened by Frank himself.

"There you are," he said. "Get the fuck in here."

He was mad.

I walked in and closed the door. Frank went straight to the bar and got behind it. He was wearing a polo shirt, a pair of brown slacks and loafers.

"Bourbon?" he asked.

"Beer," I said. I wanted to keep my head.

He got a bottle of Piels from the small refrigerator behind him, then poured himself a bourbon, obviously not willing to take the time to make a pitcher of martinis. He put the beer on the bar for me.

"Siddown," he said. "We gotta talk."

He was so angry his Jersey was coming out. I understood, because when I got that mad my Brooklyn always came out.

"You know he bought the Sands, right? Howard Hughes?"

"I know it," I said, taking a stool at the bar and grabbing the beer.

"When he has complete control, and his new tower is open, he's gonna force me out."

"You think Jack Entratter's gonna allow that, Frank?" I asked.

"He'll fire Entratter," Frank said.

"This is all gonna take time."

"Time that we have to use," he said.

"To do what?" I asked.

"To stop 'im," Frank said.

Other than Howard Hughes buying the Sands, Frank was having a great year. His album, *September of My Years,* had won the Grammy earlier in the year for Best Album of 1965. The single from that album,

"It Was a Very Good Year," won for Best Vocal Performance by a Male. Earlier in '66 his album *That's Life* and the single of the same name were top ten hits on the Billboard charts. His recording career was soaring, not to mention the recent success of his films NONE BUT THE BRAVE (which he directed), and VON RYAN'S EXPRESS, plus a cameo playing himself in THE OSCAR. The following year would see THE NAKED RUNNER, ASSAULT ON A QUEEN and TONY ROME. In addition, earlier that year he had married Mia Farrow. I had no first-hand knowledge of how the marriage was going, but his career was in high gear, and he was still only fifty-one years old. He had a lot of successful years ahead of him.

But this thing with Howard Hughes, that would eat at him.

"Frank," I said, "anybody on the strip would want you in their showrooms."

"This place has my showroom, Eddie," Frank said. "The Sands is my place." His face grew red, and his eyes and nostrils flared.

"So whataya wanna do about it?" I asked.

"We hafta stop 'im!" Frank shouted.

"That's what Jack said," I told him. "He sent me to talk to Hughes."

"And what'd he say?"

"He's lookin' for properties to buy," I said. "He might even buy the D.I."

"And what'd he ask you to do?"

"He wants me to find properties for him and talk the owners into selling."

Frank thought that over for a moment, sipped his drink, then shook his head and said, "That smug sonofabitch." He drained his glass and poured another. "So what've you been doin'?"

"The opposite," I said. "I spent early today on Fremont Street tryin' to convince everybody not to sell."

"And?"

"They didn't need me to tell 'em that," I told him. "Nobody intends to sell to Hughes."

"Yeah," he said, "nobody *intends* to sell, but he's got more money than God. *Somebody'll* take his offer."

"So what are you suggestin' we do, Frank?" I asked. "Kill 'im?"

Frank stared at me and then smiled.

"I wish I had the balls to do that, pally," he said. "I really wish I did. But you and me, Eddie, this is our town. We own it, kid. We can't let Howard Hughes take it away from us."

"I'm doin' what I can, Frank," I said. "I plan on talkin' to everybody on the strip."

"Okay, we can start there," he said. "We can both do that."

"I've got somethin' else on my plate, though."

"What's that?"

"Danny Thomas is here."

"I know that," Frank said. "We already talked. I like Danny. Me and him, we did a show with Dino in fifty-eight where we sang a medley of Academy Award nominated songs. It was a gas. He wants me to come up on stage with him tonight." He laughed. "That'll burn Hughes' ass when he hears about it."

"Did he tell you his problem?" I asked.

"Problem? Danny? What problem's he got. The guy's a fuckin' saint."

So I told him.

Chapter Fifteen

Frank listened patiently while I outlined Danny Thomas' problems with St. Jude. I thought I actually saw him calming down during the time it took me to explain.

"You know," he said, when I was done, "Danny Thomas is one of the finest men I've ever known. It figures he'd come up with somethin' like St. Jude. It stinks that somebody might be puttin' their hands in his pockets. So, if you need any help, I'm in."

"I'll let you know, Frank," I said. "So, are you gonna go up on stage with 'im tonight?"

"Yeah, why not?" Frank said. "He's a great guy, but he can't sing worth a damn. I'll have to save his act." He laughed, so I'd know he was joking.

"I guess I'll have to come and see that," I said.

"You won't wanna miss it," Frank said. "Dino might be there, too."

"Is he in town, too?" I asked. "What did you guys do, sneak in on me?"

"Naw, we came in on my plane," Frank said. "When I told Dean I was comin', he took some time off from his show and hitched a ride. I told 'im I was gonna talk to you about Hughes. He said he'd hang back. You'll be hearin' from him, or just see 'im tonight. Danny might drag him up on stage, too."

"How's Dino feel about Hughes?"

"He's got nothin' against 'im personally," Frank said, "but he doesn't want him takin' over Vegas, either."

"Vegas is changin', Frank," I said. "We might be able to slow it down, but we ain't gonna stop it. The mob's on the way out and the bean counters are on the way in."

"That's fine, Eddie," Frank said, "I just don't want Howard Hughes' beans in the pot."

"That makes two of us," I said.

***

When I left Frank's suite, I promised to stop backstage if I made it to Danny Thomas' show that night.

I thought I'd find Jerry on the casino floor, or in the Garden Room, but instead he was out front talking with three of the valets.

"Hey, Eddie," the valets said, as I came out. Several cars pulled in, and they went off to park them, waving to Jerry as they left.

"What was that about?" I asked.

"I just wanted to see what they knew about Mr. Hughes," Jerry said.

"And?"

"They had more on his man, Maheu. Looks like he's a gambler. Also, he ain't gettin' along so good with his boss, these days."

"Where'd they get that from?"

"A valet at the Desert Inn," Jerry said. "He heard them arguin' when they pulled in and turned their car over to him. He said if he had to bet, Maheu's gettin' fired pretty soon."

"I thought Maheu was Hughes' main man," I said.

"Maybe," Jerry said, as we turned and went back inside, "he'll be lookin' for a new main man soon. If you give 'im what he wants, I bet you could get that job."

"The last thing I want to do is work for Howard Hughes," I said.

"He'd pay you a boat load of money, Mr. G."

"I couldn't do it Jerry."

Jerry grinned.

"I didn't think so. What's next?"

"We're gonna pass the word on Howard Hughes," I said. "Between me and Frank, maybe we can keep him from buyin' up any more casinos."

Chapter Sixteen

We hit the Flamingo, the Sahara and the Riviera, then had dinner. While we ate, I asked Jerry if he wanted to see Danny Thomas' show, adding that Frank and Dino might be there.

"I'm in," he said, and we went.

Danny dragged Frank and Dean on stage, but they weren't kicking and screaming. He introduced them as his "very good friends," who you all might know, and the audience went wild.

The three of them sang, joked and did some very Rat Pack style things, as if they'd been doing it all their lives. But instead of doing Italian jokes about each other or black jokes about Sammy, Frank and Dino did Lebanese jokes about Danny Thomas. The audience ate it up, and Jerry laughed longer and louder than I'd ever seen him do before. The others we ended up sitting with at our table got a huge kick out of him.

After the show, I took Jerry backstage with me. Everybody was crowded into Danny Thomas' dressing room. Champagne was flowing, friends and reporters were trying to touch the three of them or get their attention. We couldn't get near them, but Dino appeared at my side and said, "Wait in the dressing room next door, pally, and we'll go out for a bite after."

Even though we had already eaten dinner, that excited Jerry, so we nodded and got out of there.

The room next door—almost identical—was eerily calm, but we could still hear the commotion next door. Dean appeared first, his hair mussed, face slick with sweat, his collar open and bowtie gone.

"Wow, it's a madhouse," he said. "I'm gonna take a quick shower."

Nothing went quick. Dean showered, then Frank slipped in, and we had to wait for him to do the same. Finally, we had to wait for the crowd to get out of Danny Thomas' dressing room so he could shower and get dressed.

When Danny finally came, wearing in a sharp grey suit that probably cost more than my whole wardrobe, he was shaking his head and grinning.

"I don't even know who most of those people are," he commented.

I had recognized some of them, people like Buddy Greco, Shirley MacLaine, Jack Jones, Buddy Rich, Bobby Troupe & Julie London, Steve Lawrence & Eydie Gormé, and more.

Frank walked up to Danny and felt the material of his jacket.

"What's with the suit, Clyde?" he asked. "We're just goin', out for a snack."

"I beg your pardon," Danny said, stepping back and adjusting his jacket, "but I have an image to uphold."

"How hard can it be to maintain a Lebanese image?" Dino asked.

Danny did that thing he always did on T.V. when "Danny Williams" is about to explode, widening his eyes.

"Excuse me if I believe my reputation is above that of some pretty-boy Dago," Danny said.

Dino's face froze, Frank raised his eyebrows and stuck out his lower lip, then the three of them started laughing.

I introduced Jerry to Danny Thomas, and then we all headed out to a limo Frank had arranged for us. Frank didn't have any members of his entourage with him—not even Jilly Rizzo—but he rarely did when he came to Vegas and hung with Dino. In the car Danny bitched about Frank always making him eat spaghetti and meatballs, so Frank told the driver to take us to the Golden Steer, which was his favorite steak house.

We all had steaks the size of Victor Mature's leg, and while some of us left enough meat on the plate to bet on, Jerry impressed everybody by leaving nothing but a clean bone.

The conversation stayed light with lots of laughs and no talk of St. Jude or Howard Hughes. That suited all of us.

We took the limo back to the Sands and everybody split up in the lobby and went to their own rooms—except for me. I went to the lounge, where the late-night act had just finished, which suited me. I wanted a few quiet minutes to wash the taste of the champagne out of my mouth.

"Bourbon," I said to the bartender.

"Comin' up, Mr. G."

When Jerry called me Mr. G. it was an obvious sign of affection from the big lug. When the employees called me that, it was a sign of respect.

"There ya go," he said, setting the glass in front of me.

"Thanks."

I sipped slowly, letting my mind drift back to Howard Hughes and what he and his money could do to Las Vegas. He was wealthy enough to buy every major casino on the strip, if he wanted to.

"Can a lady get a drink?" a woman's voice asked.

I looked to my right and saw a black-haired beauty sitting on a stool, holding a cigarette.

"And a light?" she added.

I said to the bartender, "Get the lady a drink," then picked up a book of matches from the bar and lit one for her. She leaned in, revealing an expanse of cleavage swelling from her purple dress.

"Thanks," she said, then told the bartender, "A martini, please."

"You're welcome."

She smiled and accepted the martini glass from the bartender.

"What brings you to the Sands at this hour?" I asked.

"I'm in Vegas discussing business," she said. "As for the Sands at this hour . . . I was restless, couldn't stay in my hotel room a minute longer."

I figured her for about forty-years-old, but she was a stunner, with pale skin and blood red lipstick.

"It's quiet, here," she said.

"That's why I'm here," I said. "For the quiet."

"Really?" she said, playing with her glass. "I assumed you work here. Don't you have a room for that?"

"I have a room I use when I stay, instead of goin' home," I admitted.

She sipped her drink and it made her lips shine when she lowered the glass.

"I'd like to see it," she said.

"See . . . it?" I stammered.

"Your room," she said, grabbing her purse, which she had set down on the bar. "Can we go there?"

"Do you, uh, want to know my name, first?" I asked.

"This is nothing serious, sweetie," she said. "I just need some company. Is that . . . something you'd like?"

She didn't strike me as a pro, just a woman fighting loneliness on a late Vegas night.

"That's somethin' I'd like a lot," I admitted.

She smiled. "Let's go, then."

Chapter Seventeen

I woke the next morning just in time to watch her walk naked across the room to the bathroom. Her skin seemed to glow, but her ass swayed seductively even though she didn't know I was watching. When the door to the bathroom closed behind her, I felt an odd sense of loss.

We'd had a few drinks the night before, and then gravitated to the bed. I had made love with some special women in the past—Ava Gardner topping the list—but this mystery lady was certainly right up there. At least, judging from what I could remember of the night before, and from what I had just seen.

When she came back into the room, I had a clear frontal view this time, and she was completely unabashed while also not the least bit flirtatious. She had the body of a Vegas showgirl.

"I'm sorry, but I have to get going," she said, grabbing her dress from the floor. "Last night was very nice, but—"

"—I know," I said. "Nothing serious. That's okay. I needed a distraction, as well. It was fun—and totally unexpected."

"This is just between us, right?"

"Definitely," I said. "This is not somethin' I want to share with anyone."

"You're sweet," she said, and was out the door with a wave.

Nothing but a wonderful memory for years to come . . . or so I thought, at the time.

***

I came down to the Garden Room for breakfast and found Jerry already there. He had a stack of pancakes in front of him that looked like the leaning tower.

"What happened to the diet?" I asked. "That's no way to manage your diabetes."

"My doctor says I can take a day off now and then," Jerry said. "I woke up hungry. Besides—" he tapped the syrup bottle. "—this has no sugar."

A waitress I knew on sight but not by name came by, so I read the tag on her chest.

"What can I get you, Mr. G.?" she asked.

" 'mornin', Lily," I said. "Ham-and-eggs'll do it, toast and coffee."

"Gotcha."

"Cute," Jerry said, watching her walk away.

"They're all cute, Jerry," I said. "The waitresses, the hat check girls, the cigarette girls, the dealers . . . it's part of the job."

I had just spent the night with a beautiful woman, but I wasn't sharing that.

Jerry shrugged and turned his attention back to his leaning stack.

"What're we doin' today?" Jerry asked.

"Eatin' breakfast," I said. "I'll decide what's next after we're done."

Lily came with my plate, filled my coffee cup and refilled Jerry's.

"Anything else, gentlemen?" she asked.

"Not right now, Lily," I said. "Thanks."

I started eating. We talked about the show the night before, the dinner afterward, a bit about Howard Hughes and his man, Maheu, and then I noticed Jerry looking past me.

"What?" I asked.

"You ain't gonna like this," he said.

"Damn."

"Don't turn around," he said, "just keep on eatin'."

I did like he told me. Trouble came up next to our booth and stopped.

"Eddie G.," he said.

"Detective Hargrove," I said. "I was hopin' after our last go around that you'd get fired, or at least suspended. But here you are."

"Here I am."

"Still a detective?"

He showed me his badge. I looked at the man next to him.

"I assume this is yet another new partner?"

"This is Detective Sanderson."

The man stared at me and remained silent. He was at least ten years older than Hargrove, but I had the feeling I knew who was going to do the talking.

"And here's your partner," Hargrove said, looking at Jerry. "Why am I not surprised?"

Jerry smiled at him and kept eating, but faster. He wanted to finish before Hargrove took us away from our meals.

Hargrove looked back at me.

"I could've sent a couple of patrolmen to do this, but I wanted to do it myself."

"What?" I asked. "Interrupt my breakfast?"

"That's the least of it," Hargrove said. "I need you to come with me—now!"

"Am I under arrest for somethin'?" I asked.

"Not yet."

"Do I need a lawyer?"

"Not yet."

"Am I comin', too?" Jerry asked.

"No," Hargrove said.

I cut a huge slice of ham and stuck it in my mouth.

"Okay," I said around it, standing up, "let's go."

Chapter Eighteen

I thought they'd be driving me to their office, but instead we went to the morgue. That wasn't good. I knew Jerry would go straight to Jack Entratter's office, and that Jack would probably have a lawyer sent to headquarters. He was going to be disappointed not to find me there.

I didn't say anything during the ride, and neither did they. But once I knew we were at the morgue, I was too curious not to ask.

"What's goin' on?"

Neither of them answered or turned to look at me. Sanderson was driving, but he didn't even look at me in the rearview mirror.

"Okay, fine," I said.

He parked and they got out of the sedan. Hargrove opened the back-door and said, "Get out!"

The alternative was to stay in the backseat, so I did as I was told.

"Are you gonna tell me what's goin' on?" I asked.

"Once we're inside," Hargrove said.

They kept me between them as we entered and took the elevator down to the bowels of the hospital, where the morgue was.

They led me into a room with white-tiled walls, a desk and a couple of chairs.

"Sit," Hargrove said.

I sat, they stood.

"Where were you last night?" Hargrove asked.

"When last night?"

"Why don't you just tell us everythin' you did last night," he said.

So I did. I started after dinner, when Jerry and I went to Danny Thomas' show. I told them about going backstage, about going out after, about going to the lounge, and then going to bed.

"Alone?" Hargrove asked.

"Why?"

"We need to know if anybody can corroborate your story."

"My story?" I repeated. "Just ask Danny Thomas, Frank Sinatra and Dean Martin."

"Sure, sure," Hargrove said, "your big showbiz friends, who'll swear to any lie you tell."

"Well, that shouldn't be a problem," I said, "since I haven't told any lies."

And I hadn't. I'd left something out, but that was an omission, not a lie. And I wasn't all that sure why I had omitted the lady from the story, except that she seemed to want to keep our time together between us. But we never exchanged names, so who were we going to tell?

"Look, Hargrove," I said, "want's goin' on? Why am I here?"

He looked at his partner, who didn't even blink, yet seemed to have transmitted some sort of message.

"Okay, let's go," Hargrove said. "Up!"

"Where to this time?" I asked.

"You'll see."

I got up and, once again, we walked with one of them on either side of me. Except we didn't get very far, just down the hall to a pair of double doors. Now we were in a cold room with slabs and metal drawers. Most of the slabs were empty at the moment, except for a couple that were covered with sheets. I looked around, but there was no sign of the usual white-coated attendant, just us.

I knew Hargrove would have loved to put me in one of those metal drawers, but I hoped today wasn't the day.

"Hargrove—"

"That one," he said, pointing to a slab with a sheet covered body on it.

We walked to it and stopped. He reached out, grabbed the sheet and pulled it down. It was a naked woman who had been very beautiful in life. I could vouch for that because I had slept with her the night before.

Chapter Nineteen

"Know 'er?" Hargrove asked.

"No," I said. Still not a lie, technically. I didn't know who she was.

"Nice set of tits, huh?" he said.

"A little respect would be nice."

It was Sanderson who reached out and put the sheet back over her.

"She was found dead in the front seat of her car, parked on West Tropicana," Hargrove said. "In the visor was a valet ticket from the Sands."

"So?"

"Still say you don't know 'er?" Hargrove asked.

I made a show of thinking about it.

"Let me see her face again," I said.

Sanderson reached for the sheet and revealed just her face.

"I saw her in the lounge at the Sands last night, late," I said.

"That's it?"

"I lit her cigarette."

"You know her name?"

"We weren't introduced." Again, not a lie.

"Okay, come on," Hargrove said.

"I can go now?" I asked.

"Yeah," he said, "down the hall."

They escorted me back to that white-tiled room. I felt like I was in a men's room where all the urinals and toilets had been removed.

"Sit!" Hargrove snapped.

I did.

He took a plastic bag out of his pocket. Inside was a piece of paper.

"Do you see what's written on that?" he asked, holding it in front of my face.

I did. Scrawled in an almost intelligible handwriting was my name: EDDIE GIANELLI.

"So?"

"This was in the dead woman's purse." He pulled it away and stuck it back in his pocket. "How do you explain that?"

"I can't explain it," I said.

"And you still maintain you never met the woman?"

Still not lying I said, "No, I never met her." Fucked her, yes. Met her? No!

Hargrove looked at Sanderson, who stared back with no expression. "Eddie," he said to me, "you're full of shit!"

***

They kept me there for a few hours, trying to get me to change my story. But I had stuck with it for so long there was no way I could change it and explain why I had been evasive.

Of course, one reason was I didn't like Hargrove and didn't want to cooperate with him. I felt bad for the woman, who I truly didn't know and had only spent a few hours with.

According to Hargrove she had been found strangled behind the wheel of her car, indicating that someone had been in the back seat.

"I've never been in her car," I said.

"If we find one hair of yours, or a thread from your clothes—"

"You won't."

They hadn't mentioned her name yet, obviously waiting for me to slip up and tell it to them. That wasn't going to happen because it couldn't.

Another reason I didn't admit to having spent the night with her was because, if I did, it would make me the number one suspect—if Hargrove wasn't thinking that already.

But it was time for me to ask.

"You guys want to tell me her name? Maybe that'd ring a bell with me."

They looked at each other, and again something passed between them. Maybe Hargrove had finally found a partner he clicked with. Most of them dumped him as soon as they could.

"Her name," he said, "was Susan Morrow."

I hesitated, then said, "Doesn't ring a bell."

Meanwhile, bells, whistles and klaxon horns were going off in my head.

"Was she robbed?" I asked.

"Her purse was on the front seat next to her, and her wallet was still in it." Hargrove said. "She had a couple a-hundred bucks."

So no robbery. But somebody had killed her, and maybe I knew why.

"Look," I said, "we've been here for hours. Either charge me with something or let me go."

"Charge you?" Hargrove said. "Why would I charge you, Eddie? We only brought you here to see if you could identify her."

"Then I'm free to go?"

"Free as a bird," Hargrove said, then added, "for now."

I stood up.

"Any chance of gettin' a ride back to the Sands?"

"Don't push your luck," Hargrove said.

"Never mind," I said. "I'll get a cab."

I wanted to run out of the room, but I took my time until I got out of the elevator on the main floor. Then I made a quick beeline for the door.

Susan Morrow.

Damn!

I had spent the night with the woman whose name was on the list Danny Thomas gave me. She was one of the people he suspected of skimming St. Jude money.

Chapter Twenty

I could've called Jerry to come and pick me up, but the keys to my Caddy were in my pocket. So I walked to the corner, to get away from all the official vehicles and waved down a cab.

"The Sands," I said.

"You got it!" the driver said.

I don't like coincidences. The fact that Susan Morrow had my name in her purse made me believe that meeting her at the bar had been planned. Had she also planned to seduce me? And if so, for what purpose? She had been quick to leave the hotel room the next morning. What had she accomplished? And was she, indeed, the one who was skimming money from St. Jude? See, that'd be the coincidence, if she *was* in Vegas and *wasn't* the guilty one.

***

When I got back to the Sands, I called Danny Thomas' room to see if he was available.

"Sure," he said, "I'm just makin' plans for my last show. Come on up."

"I'll be there in half an hour," I said. "I need to stop in to see Jack Entratter first."

"Fine," Danny said, "see you then."

I hung up the house phone and took the elevator to Jack Entratter's office.

"There you are!" he said, waving his arms while seated behind his desk. "We can call off the search!"

"Yes." I sat in front of his desk.

"When your buddy Jerry came up here and told me the cops took you, I sent a lawyer over to headquarters."

"They took me to the morgue. Is that coffee?" I pointed to the cup on his desk.

"Yeah, I ain't touched it. Take it."

"Thanks."

It was lukewarm, but I needed it.

"Why did they take you to the morgue."

"To identify a dead woman who had been murdered."

"Murdered! Did you know 'er?"

"No, I didn't."

"Then was Hargrove just jerkin' you around?" he asked.

"Apparently," I said, "she had my name on a piece of paper in her purse."

Jack sat back in his chair and shook his head.

"Then he had no choice but to question you."

"He kept me for hours," I said. "That part was just jerkin' me around. Where *is* Jerry, anyway?"

"I'm not sure," Jack said. "He might be with the lawyer."

"At the police station? I doubt it. I'll try his room." I stood up. Put the coffee cup back on his desk. "I've gotta go see Danny Thomas."

"About his trouble?"

"Yeah, about that," I said, and told him who the dead woman was.

***

"Susan's dead?" Danny Thomas blurted, looking as if he had been punched in the stomach. He got that pop-eyed look, but not the funny one. "How?"

"She was strangled."

"B-but, why? Was it because she was the one stealing?"

"I don't know," I said, "but she had my name in her purse. Did you tell 'er who I was? What I was doin'?"

"No!" he said. "Eddie, why would I do that?"

"I'm just checkin'," I said. "Somebody told her." I didn't tell him that I was with her last night. I was keeping that to myself so it wouldn't get back to Hargrove. I needed him to keep looking for her killer without looking at me.

"What about the other two?" Danny asked. "Have you spoken to them, yet?"

"Not yet," I said, "but I will."

"Maybe this has nothing to do with St. Jude," he said, hopefully.

"Danny, wouldn't that be too much of a coincidence?" I asked, since I'd given the matter some thought. "Why else would she be in Vegas, looking for me?"

"This is getting out of hand," he said. He was seated on the sofa in his suite, his hands clasped between his knees. "I wouldn't have wanted Susan dead, even if she was stealing. I would've fired her."

"She was your public relations person?" I asked.

"Initially," he said, "but later she got more involved. She said she wanted to do whatever she could to help."

"And the two men, Hector Dominguez and Clarence Foster, are doctors, right?"

"Yes. But Clarence is more of an administrator."

"And Dominguez?"

"A surgeon."

"And they live in Memphis?"

"Yes," Danny said. "Will you still help me, Eddie? I'm sorry Susan's dead, but if she's not the one who was stealing, I still have my problem." He sat back and his face softened. "You know, I'd put my daughter Marlo in charge, but she's got her hands full with That Girl, right now. I can't ask her to give up a hit show."

I didn't know what to say to that.

"Your last show is tonight?"

"That's right."

"Let me have today to try and wrap my head around this, Danny. I'll talk to you in the mornin'."

"That's fair," he said. "Thank you, Eddie."

I left Danny Thomas's suite and went to the room where I'd spent the night with Susan Morrow. At the very least, I needed a shower after spending time down at the morgue.

Chapter Twenty-One

I took a shower, then prowled around the room to see if maybe Susan Morrow had left anything behind. After all, she'd orchestrated a night in my room. There had to be a reason other than my sparkling charm. But there was nothing, not even any indication that she had been there. Had she just been checking me out, for some reason? Slept with me just to get in my room? If that was the case, she hadn't found anything, because all my personal belongings were in my house. I didn't even have a clean shirt or underwear and had to put yesterday's back on.

I used the phone to try Jerry's room first. When he didn't answer I left and went down to the lobby. Almost immediately I saw the big guy coming toward me.

"Mr. G.," he said. "I was worried."

"Nothin' to worry about, Jerry," I said. "Hargrove took me to the morgue."

"The morgue? What the hell for?"

"To see if I could identify a dead woman."

"Why you?"

"Seems she had my name in her purse," I said. "You want to get some lunch?"

"Yeah, sure. The Garden Room?"

"Not here," I said. "Someplace outside, maybe just a hot dog stand?"

"That's good enough for me."

We left the hotel and got in my Caddy in the parking lot, Jerry behind the wheel.

"You didn't wanna talk inside," he said.

"No, I didn't. Never mind the hot dog stand," I said. "We can get a foot long over near the Stardust."

"Suits me."

***

We parked in the Westwood Ho parking lot, which surrounded the two-story motel-like rooms, which in turn surrounded several pools. Inside the one-story casino we were able to get a couple of cheap foot long hot dogs and a couple of beers. The Westwood Ho would build a larger casino building in 1971.

We stood at a tall tabletop that had no chairs.

"So," Jerry said, "did you know the woman?"

"Yes and no."

"What's that mean?" he asked, as some green relish dripped down his chin. He grabbed a napkin and caught it before it got on his shirt.

"It means I slept with her last night."

He stopped chewing, stared at me for a moment, then grinned and said, "You dog!" and started chewing again.

"No, I'm not a dog, I'm an idiot," I said, and told him the story.

"Then she must've been killed soon after she left you," he said, when I was done.

"The car," I said.

"What about it?"

"It must've been a rental car," I said. She doesn't live here, she lives in Tennessee, and I doubt she drove her own car here."

"Maybe she rented it at the airport," he suggested.

"That's a good thought," I said, "and one the police already would've had."

"Yeah," he said, "but you've got connections."

"You're right, I do," I said. "I'll have to make a call to the airport when we get back."

"If anybody remembers her," Jerry said, "maybe they'll also remember if somebody was with her."

"If she drove the car here, the valets would remember," I said. "She was a beautiful woman."

"Okay," he said, "when we get back you make your call, and I'll talk to the valets."

***

When we got back to the Sands, I went to the house phones while Jerry talked with the valets. I called a contact I had at McCarran Airport, a baggage handler. I used to know the head of security, but that position had been changed since I was instrumental in his losing his job.

"Hey, Eddie, what's up?" Al Corley asked.

I explained my situation to Al, telling him as much as I thought he needed to know. It would have been easier to talk to the security head, but I hadn't bonded in any way with him, yet. But Al and I knew each other for a few years, since he'd come to town, gotten the job at McCarran, and started gambling at some of the casinos on the strip, including the Sands. He owed me.

"A beautiful brunette," he said, probably writing it down, "by what name?"

"Susan Morrow."

"What's she done?" he asked. "Reneged on a marker?"

"You're a smart man," I said.

"All right," he promised, "I'll see if anyone here remembers her, or if she rented a car at any of the stalls."

"Get back to me as soon as you can, will ya, Al?" I asked.

"Sure thing, Eddie," Al said. "Quick as I can."

I hung up, left the house phones and went to the lounge to wait for Jerry.

Chapter Twenty-Two

It was afternoon, time for beer, not bourbon. I was halfway through one when Jerry came in. I waved at the bartender to bring the big guy one.

"Thanks," Jerry said, taking a stool.

"Anything from the valets?"

"The ones who are on now don't remember her," Jerry said. "I'll go out again when the new shift starts."

"It was pretty late when she came into the lounge," I said. "She could've parked the car herself. We might have to start checking hotel registrations."

"If she was here to gamble money she stole from St. Jude, wouldn't it be dumb of her to use her own name to rent a car, or a room?"

"Good point, Jerry," I said. "We'll have to circulate her name and description."

"You know we're gonna run into the cops at some point," Jerry said. "Your buddy, Hargrove, ain't gonna like us lookin' inta this."

"I'll just have to explain we're not tryin' to find out who killed her," I said, "just if she's the one who was stealin' from St. Jude."

"You think he's gonna buy that?"

"Probably not," I said. "So, we'll have to avoid him as long as we can."

"What about the shamus?" Jerry said. "Ya gotta fill him in, no?"

"Yeah, we do," I said. "Hopefully, he's still in town."

"Where would he go?"

"Who knows?" I said. "With what I asked him to do, he could be in Memphis, Nashville, or Atlantic City."

"Nashville?" Jerry made a face. "Who'd wanna go there? Ain't they all hayseeds?"

"Not all." I waved at the bartender. "I better try to call 'im."

I signaled the bartender to bring me a phone, and dialed Danny's office.

"He's not here, Eddie," Penny said.

"Is he in town?"

"Yeah, he is," she said. "He was gonna leave tomorrow, though."

"I've gotta talk to him before he leaves, Penny," I said. "Would you ask him to call me, or come and see me? It's important."

"Sure, Eddie, I'll tell 'im," she said. "Are you all right?"

"I'm fine," I said. "It has to do with business."

"Okay, Eddie," she said, sounding a little miffed that I wouldn't fill her in more, "I'll tell 'im you called."

"Little Penny upset?" Jerry asked as I hung up.

"What makes you ask that?"

"You didn't give her nuthin'," Jerry said. "She's the kinda girl who likes to be involved."

"You're right," I said, "but I'm not spreadin' this around. Danny Thomas doesn't want this gettin' out."

"Don't blame 'im," Jerry said. "He won't get any donations that way. So what's next?"

"More calls, but not from here," I said. "I'll use one of the office phones upstairs."

"You want me to make calls?"

"No," I said, "I'll be callin' in favors."

"Okay, then," Jerry said, "I'll stay down here, wait for the new shift of valets to come in."

"Good idea," I said. "I'll find you when I'm done, and we'll get some dinner."

"Works for me, Mr. G.," Jerry said.

I left Jerry there, finishing his drink, and went up to the hotel and casino offices.

***

There was always an empty desk available and the girls in the office never minded me sitting and using the phone. They knew I was usually doing something directly for Jack Entratter.

I called the front desk and told them to transfer any calls for me up to the office phone. Then I dialed a few numbers that didn't produce anything helpful. I was between calls when the phone rang, and it was Danny Bardini.

"Penny's pissed at you," he said.

"Sorry," I said, "I'm playin' this close to the vest."

"What's up?"

I told him about Susan Morrow's murder, and he realized how it affected the investigation.

"You know that makes the other two names on the list suspects, right?" he asked, when I was done. "Plus Danny Thomas."

"Well, right now Hargrove knows nothing about her connection to St. Jude and Danny Thomas."

"That won't last," Danny said. "Whataya want me to do, Eddie?"

"Concentrate on those other two names," I said. "Let's see if they've been anywhere near Vegas."

"Are we lookin' into the theft, or the murder?" he asked.

"It's gotta be connected, don't you think, Danny?"

"I feel the same way about coincidences that you do, buddy," he said. "You know that. You better warn Mr. Thomas that the cops might be talkin' to him soon. Her involvement with St. Jude ain't gonna be a secret for long."

"I'm on it," I said. "Talk to you later."

"Soon as I get back from Nashville," he said. "I'm thinkin' that's the place to start."

"Watch out for the hayseeds," I said. "Accordin' to Jerry, that's all that's there."

"Not a problem," he said. "You know what a big Jimmy Dean fan I am."

He hung up laughing, because he knew that I knew how much he hated country music.

Chapter Twenty-Three

The next time the phone rang it was Dino.

"Sorry I haven't called you, pally, but Frank wanted to talk to you first," his smooth as butter voice told me.

Talking to Dean Martin always reminded me that no matter how cool everybody said Frank Sinatra was, Dino was cool without trying. It just oozed from his pores, even during all those years he was Jerry Lewis' straight man. Jerry had always said Dean was the most naturally funny man he ever knew.

"I've heard about Howard Hughes bein' in town," Dean said. "Anythin' I can do?"

"You could have him killed," I said.

He laughed and said, "You got the wrong dago for that, pally."

"Actually," I said, "between Frank and me, I think we can pretty much kill any chances Howard Hughes has of takin' over Vegas, but if I need you, I'll give you a call."

"You know where I'll be."

"The golf course."

"You got it," he said. "Call me if you've got time for dinner."

"I'll do that, Dino. Thanks."

We hung up.

One of the secretaries brought me a cup of coffee and a donut. She was middle-aged and there was nothing flirtatious in the gesture. She was just sharing, as one of the other girls had brought in a box of donuts.

"Jelly," she told me, "the kind you like, Eddie."

"Thanks, Marge."

"Just tryin' to make you feel like one of the girls," she said, and went back to her desk.

I bit into the donut, which was so chock full of jelly that it got on my cheeks. I used a napkin to clean my face and washed the mouthful down with a sip of coffee, while considering my next call.

Dino talking about having dinner gave me an idea. When you wanted to talk to somebody in charge, you didn't always call the boss. For instance, somebody wanting to get something done in the Sands wouldn't necessarily call Jack Entratter, but they'd call me. So what I did was to make a list of my counterparts in some of the other casinos. Then I called them and made arrangements for lunch or dinner over the next few days. That seemed to me the more useful move than simply walking in off the street.

By the time I was done with my calls Jerry had appeared in the office, attracting the attention of the girls who were awed by his size, and then charmed by his manner. In the end, Jerry also got a donut and a cup of coffee as he sat down across from me.

"You're not supposed to be eating that," I said, as he bit into a frosted donut.

"Ya didn't expect me ta be rude, didja?" he asked. "You got some jelly on yer chin."

I cleaned it off with a napkin and asked, "Did you get anythin' from the valets?"

"Nobody seems to remember her drivin' in," he said, "so she probably parked her own car."

"Which would've made it easy for somebody to sneak into the backseat and wait for her."

"Right. What've you got?"

I told him I had lunch and dinner plans for the next few days.

"You do?" he asked. "Or we do?"

"You can come along, if you want," I said. "In fact, Frank might even be at a few."

"Lunch or dinner with Mr. S. sounds good to me," he said.

"And I heard from Dino," I said. "He's playin' golf but offered to help if he could."

"Seems to me with Mr. S. and Dino on your side, you'd have Hughes beat."

"Don't forget his money," I said. "It's hard to beat all that money, but we're gonna try."

"Why don't he just stay in the movie business, and find us some more broads like that Jane Russell?" Jerry said.

"I'm with you there, Jerry," I agreed.

"You got more calls to make?" he asked.

"Not today," I said. "We might as well go downstairs."

We thanked the girls for the phone, donuts and coffee and headed for the elevator. When we got to the first floor and the elevator doors opened, I stepped out first and immediately saw Hargrove walking across the lobby.

"Stay in the elevator, Jerry," I said. "Hargrove's comin'. Just go back up."

"Gotcha, Mr. G."

The elevator doors closed before Hargrove reached me, so he never saw Jerry.

"Gianelli," he said, "a word."

I could've given him the first word that came to mind, but that would've just antagonized him.

"Whataya need, Detective?" I asked.

"Let's go someplace and talk."

"The Garden Room," I said, and led the way.

Chapter Twenty-Four

We sat in a booth, but I waved the waitress away, not wanting to offer Hargrove anything.

"What's on your mind, Hargrove?"

"You, Eddie," Hargrove said. "You and that dead broad."

"What about her?"

"I want you to tell me what she was doin' here, and why she was lookin' for you?"

I liked the question. It meant he hadn't gotten very far in his investigation. It didn't matter that I'd forgotten to warn Danny Thomas the cops might be talking to him, because that wasn't going to happen soon.

"I told you, Detective," I said, "I didn't know the woman."

"Yeah, I know you told me that," he growled. Then he looked around. "Where's the goddamned waitress. I could use a cup of coffee."

"Well," I said, "why don't you have your coffee while I go back to work." I stood up and gave the waitress a wave. "Get Detective Hargrove a cup of coffee and put it on my tab."

"Yes, Eddie," Gina said.

"Not so fast, Eddie!" Hargrove snapped. "I didn't say I was done with you."

"You got another question?"

"Siddown!" he snapped.

I sat. He pointed a finger at me.

"Now that woman came to this casino to see you," he said. "And I wanna know why."

I was in good shape as long as he kept asking me questions that I could answer without actually out-and-out lying to the police.

"I don't know why, Hargrove," I said. "I told you. I didn't know the woman."

"We discovered she's got a connection to St. Jude Hospital." Sure, that had to happen. "Ain't that the one Danny Thomas started?"

"Yes."

"And he's here at the Sands," Hargrove said. "Maybe she was comin' here to see him."

"Then why was my name in her purse?"

"Too bad she's not alive for us to ask."

"So now you think she wasn't lookin' for me?" I asked.

"Don't fuck with me, Eddie," he said. "She was lookin' for you, and I'm gonna find out why. But I also wanna talk to Danny Thomas. You're gonna set it up for me."

"It's late, and I don't know where he is," I said.

"Ain't he got a show tonight?"

"Yeah, his last one," I said, "but I don't know what his pre-show routine is. You'll have to talk to him, tomorrow afternoon."

He stood up and spat, "Noon! Set it up. And don't fuck with me."

"You said that already," I pointed out. "I'll do what I can."

"Hey, you're Eddie Gianelli, the fix-it man," Hargrove said. "Make it happen!"

As he started away I said, "Hargrove."

"What?"

"You find out anythin' from her car?"

"She rented it at an Avis counter in Los Angeles," Hargrove said, "then drove it here. I guess she didn't want any record of her comin' in at the airport." He pointed at me. "She was up to no good, Eddie, and it got her killed. Maybe you oughtta keep that in mind."

"I will."

Hargrove turned and strode out of the room.

Jerry must've been nearby, waiting for Hargrove to leave, because moments later he walked in and sat across from me.

"What did he want?"

"He picked up on Susan Morrow's connection to St. Jude. He wants to talk to Danny Thomas."

"You can set that up."

"I can," I agreed, "but do I want to? I could let Danny get on a plane tomorrow and go home, but then I'd be doin' just what Hargrove warned me not to do."

"What's that?"

"Fuck with him."

Chapter Twenty-Five

"I hate to admit it, but he's right, you know," Jerry said after I told him about my conversation with Detective Hargrove.

"About what?"

"If she didn't want any record of her flyin' into Vegas," Jerry said, "then she was up to no good."

"I guess I can call off my guy at the airport," I said. "He's not gonna find out anythin'."

"So whatta we do?"

"There's still gotta be someplace she was stayin'," I said. "If we can find her room, maybe we can find somethin' there."

"And how do we do that?"

"I'll put the word out," I said. "Carhops, desk clerks, valets . . . somebody's got to have seen somethin'."

"And while we're waitin' to hear about that?"

"Keep talkin' to the casino owners," I said, "tryin' to make sure nobody sells to Howard Hughes."

"Money talks, ya know," he said, with a shrug. "If he offers enough . . ."

"Sometimes, Jerry," I said, "you say the smartest things."

I started out of the Garden Room.

He followed behind me, asking, "What'd I say?"

***

Before I could get back to the casino owners, I had to talk to Danny Thomas again. I called from the front desk and found him in his room.

"Come on up," he said. "I've got some coffee going here."

"Three cups worth?" I said. "I've got a friend with me."

"Bring 'im," he said, and we hung up.

Jerry and I took the elevator to Danny Thomas' floor and knocked on his door.

"Come on in," Danny said. "Coffee?"

"Sure," I said.

He went to the bar in his suite, poured three cups from the pot there. He was wearing a polo shirt, trousers, and a pair of loafers. It was one of the few times I'd seen him out of a suit.

"What's on your mind?" he asked.

"I just had a visit from a Las Vegas Police Detective," I said, "the one who's workin' on Susan Morrow's murder."

"Has he found out anything?"

"Yes," I said, "he knows about her connection to St. Jude. He wants to talk to you."

"Oh," Danny said. "When?"

"Tomorrow mornin'," I said. "Unless you want me to put him off so you can fly out."

"Ah no," Danny said, "that would just get you in trouble. I'll talk to him before I check out. Just bring him up when he gets here."

"I'll bring him up," I said, "but I'll call first."

"Suit yourself," Danny said. "I'll be ready." He looked at Jerry. "Is he always so talkative?"

"He's afraid he'll start gushing," I said. "He liked your show."

"Ah," Danny said, "well, always happy to meet a fan."

"I like Sherry Jackson," Jerry said.

"Who doesn't?" Danny said and laughed.

"Before I go," I said to Danny, "let me bounce somethin' off you."

"Go ahead."

"What if Susan Morrow wasn't the one skimmin' from St. Jude?" I suggested. "What if she knew who was, and that's what got her killed?"

"So that's why she was here," Danny said. "But . . . why was she looking for you? Why not me?"

"I don't know," I said. "But if that's the case, we're back where we started, lookin' for whoever was stealin' from you."

"St. Jude," Danny said, "not me."

"Right," I said, "that's what I meant."

"So what are you going to do next?"

"Keep lookin' into the other two, Dominguez and Foster."

"I hate thinking it was one of them," Danny said. "I trusted them."

"Like you trusted Susan?"

"Yes, like I trusted Susan."

"Well, I've got my buddy Bardini on the other two," I said. "Meanwhile, Jerry and I will keep tryin' to find out what Susan Morrow wanted."

"How do you plan to do that?"

"We're gonna find out where she was stayin'," I said. "I'll see you tomorrow with Detective Hargrove, Danny."

"Look," he said, walking us to the door, "I'm in your hands, Eddie. What do you want me to tell this detective?"

"I don't think the truth will hurt," I said. "Tell him you believe somebody's been skimmin' from St. Jude and see where he goes with that."

"And if he asks about you?"

"Just tell 'im you asked for my help."

"Okay," Danny said, as he opened the door to his room. "I'll see you fellas tomorrow."

As we walked to the elevator Jerry asked, "Do you think he'd introduce me to Sherry Jackson?"

"No," I said, "but maybe Angela Cartwright."

"Ah," Jerry scoffed, she's just a kid . . ."

95

Chapter Twenty-Six

The Caddy was in the parking lot, so we headed there, but one of the valets called out to Jerry.

"I'll catch up, Mr. G.," he said.

"Okay."

I went on to the Caddy. When I got there, I saw two guys looking it over. Then I saw a third on the other side.

"This your car?" one asked.

"That's right."

"Nice ride," he said. The other two just stared at me—hard. I got the message and was wishing Jerry was with me.

The two quiet ones stood between me and my car. The third guy started running his hands over it.

"Thanks," I said, "but I've got to get goin'."

"Do you?" the third man asked. "Hey, guys, he's gotta get goin'." They didn't move.

"Hey, guys, come on," the third man said. "Let the man get into his car."

Grudgingly, the two men parted, allowing me to pass between them. When one of them tried to grab my arms and pin them behind me, I was ready. I stomped on his foot and spun away from them, but the third man came around the car and got behind me. He did pin my arms back. The other man stepped forward and punched me in the gut. The man I stomped was still hopping around in pain when Jerry came up behind him, grabbed him by the collar and belt and tossed him halfway across the parking lot.

I tried stomping again, this time the guy behind me, but he danced around avoiding it. That loosened his hold on me, though, and I managed to pull away so I could turn and throw a punch. He ducked it and then we both saw the second man also go flying across the parking lot. That left the third man facing me and Jerry, who came over and stood beside me.

"You're lookin' for trouble, Gianelli," the man said. "Mind your own business."

He turned and ran, following the other two who had already started running. If they were armed, they were apparently told not to kill me.

"What the hell was that about, Mr. G.?" Jerry asked.

"One of two things, Jerry," I said, rubbing my stomach, "only one of two things."

***

I had a dinner date with Frank and Jay Sarno, who had built and recently opened Caesar's Palace. Sarno was a well-known developer who had built hotels in Atlantic City and California. Caesar's Palace was his first property in Las Vegas, but not his last. About a half a dozen years later he'd also open Circus Circus.

We met Frank out in front of the Golden Steer, and he didn't mind Jerry being along, at all. "Never know when you'll need some muscle," he said, with a disarming smile.

Inside we saw Sarno already seated, with a martini in front of him. He lifted it to us as we approached. We sat and introduced Jerry, and then I let Frank do most of the talking. Sarno assured us that he had no intention of selling out to Howard Hughes or anyone else. After all, he had just opened Caesar's Palace.

We ate dinner and then Sarno said he had to leave for another late meeting.

"Don't worry," he said, as he stood. "Not about me, anyway."

97

"Why?" I said. "What've you heard?"

"Just that Hughes has feelers out," Sarno said, "and some people might be listening."

He waved and left. Frank called the waiter over.

"Three more, pally," he said.

"Yes, Mr. Sinatra."

The waiter brought fresh martinis for me and Frank, and a beer for Jerry.

"Whataya think?" Frank asked.

"I don't think Sarno's gonna sell," I said. "The Palace is too new."

"What about those feelers he mentioned?"

"We knew that, already," I pointed out. "And people listenin' doesn't necessarily mean they're gonna sell.

"But Hughes asked you to ask around," Frank reminded me. "Why's he puttin' out these feelers?"

"Could be they already heard that I've been tryin' to talk people out of sellin'. Or it could be Maheu who's puttin' the word out," I said. "I could talk to him, again."

"*We* could talk to him," Frank said.

"All of us?" Jerry asked.

"Yeah, big guy, all of us," Frank said. "But I'm just sayin' talk, get it?"

"I get it, Mr. S.," Jerry assured him.

Frank sat back.

"So what else is goin' on?" he asked. "Eddie, you looked uncomfortable when you got here. What's up, pally?"

I told him what happened in the Sands parking lot.

"What'd they want?" he asked.

"Apparently to warn me off."

"Hughes sent them?"

"I don't know," I said. "Maybe Maheu did."

"Well, is there somethin' else they'd be warnin' you about?"

"The only other thing I'm workin' on is Danny Thomas' problem," I said, "and now that's turned into a murder."

"What?"

I told him about Susan Morrow being killed.

"We don't know if she was skimmin'," I went on, "or if she knew who was skimmin' and they killed 'er."

"Jesus," Frank said. "So maybe her killer sent those guys after you?"

"Maybe."

"It's a good thing Big Jerry came along when he did," Frank said.

"We were walkin' out there together, but Jerry got called back," I said. "I wonder what would've happened if we'd both walked up on them?"

"Did they have guns?" Frank asked.

"I don't know," I said. "If they did, they never went for 'em."

"It might've been different if Jerry was with you from the beginnin'."

"It might've," I said. "I'm gonna talk to Maheu. He might've sent those guys after me without Hughes knowin'."

"Why?"

"That's what I'll ask 'im."

"Maybe you should ask Hughes," Frank said.

"I don't wanna talk to him again," I said. "Not yet anyway."

"I don't blame you." Frank looked at his watch. "I gotta go back to the hotel and call Mia."

Frank was married to Mia Farrow at the time. A lot of folks wondered what that was all about. There was a thirty-year difference between them, but I never asked.

"Okay," I said, "we can drive you back."

"That's okay," Frank said, "I got a car and driver outside." He stood up. "The bill's taken care of. I'll see you guys tomorrow."

"Goodnight, Mr. S.," Jerry said.

Frank walked out, all eyes in the place following him.

***

Jerry didn't drink his second beer and I left most of my second martini. But we stuck around for a few minutes after Frank left.

"What now?" he asked.

I checked my watch.

"It's too late to go looking for Maheu," I said. "I'll find him in the mornin'."

"Where?"

"I'll bet he'll be hanging around the D.I.," I said. "If I walk in, he might find me."

"Us," Jerry said. "After what happened in the parkin' lot, Mr. G., I ain't about to let you go anywhere alone."

"Jerry—"

"Next time they might use rods," Jerry said. "And I'm packin', remember."

Whenever Jerry was heeled, he carried a .45 the size of a small cannon.

"Yeah, okay," I said. "Good point. Let's get back to the Sands."

We left the restaurant, climbed into the Caddy and drove back. It was dark when we got there, and we kept a sharp eye out as we walked across the parking lot. I kept thinking what Jerry said about them using guns next time. If Maheu or Hughes had sent them, I doubted it. But if they were connected to Susan Morrow's murder, then who knew?

There were no messages waiting for me when we got back to the lobby. I told Jerry to go ahead to his room and get some rest while I took a turn around the casino, but he insisted on staying with me.

One turn around the floor was enough to determine that everything was fine, so we decided on a night cap in the lounge before turning in.

Chapter Twenty-Seven

I stayed overnight in the hotel and woke early the next morning to get down to the lobby and wait for Hargrove. When I got out of the elevator, Jerry was already there. He meant it when he said he wasn't going to let me go anywhere by myself.

" 'mornin', Jerry."

"We got time for breakfast?"

"You do," I said. "I'll go up to Danny's room with Hargrove. You go to the Garden Room, and I'll meet you there. I still don't want Hargrove to know you're around."

"Well," he said, "I guess if you're with him you'll be all right."

"I'm sure I will be. Now scram, before he gets here."

Jerry walked across the room to the casino steps, but he waited there, staying out of sight and watching me until Hargrove arrived. And then he was gone.

Hargrove was alone, no partner. I didn't ask why. I knew he'd never had a partner who liked him.

"Let's go," he said. "I wanna get this over with."

We got in the elevator.

"Do you think you'll be able to be civil to Danny Thomas?" I asked him. "He's a very important man, you know."

"Because he's on television?" Hargrove snorted.

"He's much more than that."

"You mean the St. Jude dodge?"

"It's not a dodge," I said. "He's really trying to do some good."

"Well, I see he's got you convinced," Hargrove said.

I decided to let Hargrove make a fool of himself. It'd be interesting to see how much Danny would put up with.

When we got to his door I knocked, and Danny Thomas answered with a big smile.

"Eddie, right on time," he said. "And this must be Detective . . ."

". . . Hargrove," I said.

"Right, right," Danny said. "Come on in."

We went in and he closed the door then turned to face us. He was casually dressed in slacks and a short sleeve, button-down shirt.

"Coffee? Or something stronger?"

"Nothin', thanks," Hargrove said. "I just have some questions to ask you, Mr. Thomas. I won't take up too much of your time."

"I've got about three hours before my plane leaves, Detective," Danny Thomas said. We all sat down, Danny on the sofa, and Hargrove and I in an armchair each. "What would you like to know?"

"You knew Susan Morrow," Hargrove began.

"Yes."

"How well?"

"Pretty well, or so I thought," Danny said. "To hear that she'd been killed was a shock."

"Do you know what she was doing in Vegas?"

"Not a clue," Danny said.

"She never mentioned that she'd be comin' here?"

"Not a word."

"Did she know you'd be here?"

"I'm not sure she knew my schedule," Danny said. "My show business activities were really none of her concern. We usually only spoke about St. Jude."

"Right, right, the hospital. What was her job there?"

"Well, she was on a board of three people who ran it for me," Danny said. "But I was considering cutting that down to one."

"And were you gonna pick her?"

"I hadn't decided yet."

"Could she have been here in Vegas to try to convince you to choose her?"

"That's a possibility, I suppose, but as I said, I don't know if she even knew I was here."

"You think you and her both being in Vegas was a coincidence?" Hargrove asked.

"That would be some coincidence, wouldn't it?"

"I think so."

"So you think she was here to see me," Danny said.

"Mr. Thomas," Hargrove said, "I need you not to leave town, just yet."

"But I'm done here, and I've got shows to do—"

"You'll have to postpone them," Hargrove said. "This is a murder inquiry, and you're . . . well, a suspect."

Danny's eyes did that wide thing.

"You think I killed 'er?"

"Let's just say I want you to stay here a while longer, in case I need you," Hargrove said.

"Look, Detective," Danny said, "I didn't have anything to do with Susan's murder, and if I have to stay here in Vegas a while longer to prove it to you, I will."

"Thank you," Hargrove said.

To this point I was surprised at how decent Hargrove had been acting.

"You said she was on a panel of three running St. Jude?" Hargrove said.

"That's right."

Hargrove took out a pad and a pen.

"Could you give me the other names and their contact information?"

"Of course."

From memory Danny reeled off names, addresses and phone numbers.

"And these gents are?"

"They're both doctors, but Clarence is more of an administrator, while Hector is a surgeon."

"And what was Susan Morrow's job?"

"She mostly did public relations."

"Thank you," Hargrove said, closing his pad. "Now, if you can think of anything I should know, I'd like you to call me." He opened the pad again, scribbled his number, tore the page off and handed it to Danny. "Okay?"

"Of course," Danny said. "I'll do anything I can."

"Thank you," Hargrove said, standing up. As I stood, he waved at me and said, "I'll show myself out, Eddie. You stay here and assure Mr. Thomas that he's doing the right thing by staying here, and not crossing me."

Hargrove shook Danny's hand and said, "I enjoyed your Make Room for Daddy show." Which surprised the hell out of me.

Hargrove left and Danny sat back down on the couch, heavily.

"Does he really think I might've killed Susan?" he asked.

"It's his job to think that, Danny," I said, "but I doubt he believes it. He's probably more sure I did it."

"Oh, because she had your name in her purse."

"Right."

"And why did I get the feeling he was acting?"

"Because he was," I said. "He's usually much more of a scumbag than that."

"Except at the end, that remark about crossing him," Danny said. "He wasn't acting, then."

"No."

"Well, I guess you'll arrange for me to keep this suite a few more days?"

"I'll take care of it when I go downstairs," I said, "and I'll let Jack Entratter know."

"He'll probably try to squeeze another show out of me," Danny said. "Jack's not one to miss an opportunity."

"No, he's not."

Danny walked with me to the door.

"What are you doing the rest of the day?" he asked.

"I have some errands to run, but Dino's here and he'd probably love to play golf with you."

"Hey! That's a great idea," Danny said. "I'll call his room. Thanks, Eddie."

We shook hands and I headed for the elevator.

Chapter Twenty-Eight

Jerry was working on a stack of pancakes when I got to the Garden Room.

"How'd it go?" Jerry asked.

"Remarkably well," I said, sliding into the booth across from him. "Hargrove was . . . decent to Danny. I'm surprised he had that in him."

"Maybe it's just you and me he don't like," Jerry suggested.

"I doubt that," I said. "Remember, he's had a lot of different partners. No, I guess he's got it in him to be a decent human being, he just never lets it out."

Gina came over and I ordered ham-and-eggs. She smiled and flounced away in that way many of the girls who work Vegas do. They know what they're doing, and it increases their tips. Women's lib had not yet hit the strip.

Over breakfast we discussed our options on how to proceed in each of the matters we were involved in: Susan Morrow and Howard Hughes.

"I'm still waitin' for some word on where Susan Morrow might've been stayin'," I said. "The car's a bust if she rented it in L.A."

"And Hughes?"

"I figure to go over to the D.I. and find Maheu. I want to see what he has to say about sending those bully boys to scramble my brains or worse."

"I'm comin' along," Jerry said.

"I know it," I said. "In fact, I'm countin' on it."

***

It wasn't hard to find Robert Maheu, all we had to do was show up in the lobby of the D.I.

"Now what?" Jerry asked.

"We wait. It won't take long."

It didn't. We drifted into the casino, watched some craps, played some roulette, and then Maheu came up behind us.

"Mr. Hughes isn't expecting you," he said.

I didn't turn. I put my last five-dollar chip on number fifteen.

"I'm not here to see Hughes, I'm here to see you," I said.

"Well," he said, "we can't talk here. Let's go to the lobby."

He walked away. I turned to follow and Jerry said, "Mr. G., your number came up."

I looked at the wheel. The little white ball was sitting in the number fifteen. At thirty-seven to one that was a hundred and eighty-five bucks. Nothing to sneeze at.

"Grab my chips, will ya, Jerry?"

He collected my chips in his huge hands and followed me to the lobby.

Maheu was waiting by the elevators.

"How about the Sky Room?" he asked.

"Fine," I said. It wouldn't be that busy at this early hour.

In the late forties and early fifties "bomb parties" used to be held in the Sky Room. People could drink and watch the testing detonations in the desert from a safe distance. It was Las Vegas' way of trying to maintain its' "Atomic City" nickname.

As we got off the elevator Jerry was stuffing my chips into his pockets. Maheu got a table by the windows so we could look out over the strip. Maheu and I ordered bourbon, while Jerry had a beer which I knew he'd only drink about half.

"What's on your mind, Eddie?" Maheu asked. He had made no comment about Jerry accompanying us and wasn't even giving the big guy a look.

"I'm guessin' by now Hughes knows I'm not scoutin' locations for him to purchase."

"He's heard," Maheu said. "Apparently you and Sinatra are trying to block his purchases. It's not going to work, you know."

"Now you're gonna tell me money talks," I predicted.

"I don't have to," he said. "If anybody knows that, you do."

"Three torpedoes tried to rearrange my face in the Sands parking lot yesterday," I said. "You wouldn't happen to know anythin' about that, would you?"

"You really think Mr. Hughes does business that way?" Maheu asked.

"Maybe he doesn't," I said, "but you might. I get the feelin' he tells you what he wants done, but not how to do it. That's up to you."

"He does have confidence in me," Maheu said. "You don't look much worse for wear."

"Jerry, here, persuaded them to give it up," I said. "A couple of your goons might be feelin' it."

"I see." He looked at Jerry for the first time. "So he's your body-guard now?"

"More like a shadow," Jerry said. "Where Mr. G. goes, I go, and so does my forty-five."

"Ah," Maheu said, "a gunsel."

"More than anything else," I said, "Jerry's my friend. He just wouldn't like it if I got hurt. If somethin' did happen, I don't know what he'd do."

Maheu looked at Jerry again. The guy just gave him a baleful stare.

"Threats, Eddie?" Maheu asked.

I gave him something from my Brooklyn childhood.

"I'm just sayin', Maheu."

Maheu sipped his drink, then said, "I'll keep that in mind, Eddie."

"Do you think Mr. Hughes will want to see me again?" I asked.

"Are you asking for an audience?"

"No," I said, "I think my intentions are clear."

"As are his."

"Are they?"

"Oh yes," Maheu said, "negotiations have already started for him to purchase the Desert Inn. Then he'll start looking elsewhere."

It seemed like Frank and I were going to have to up our timetable.

I pushed away my drink, virtually untouched. Jerry did the same with his beer and we stood up.

"I assume these will be charged to Mr. Hughes' room."

Maheu raised his glass to us and drank.

Chapter Twenty-Nine

We drove back to the Sands. The marquee said DANNY THOMAS, ONE MORE NIGHT. Below that, in smaller print, it said: MAYBE FRANK! MAYBE DEAN!

"Looks like Entratter convinced Danny to do one more show while he's bein' kept here by the police," I said, as we pulled into the lot.

The "Maybes" were usually reserved for nights when one of the guys was playing. It'd say FRANK SINATRA, and then underneath MAYBE DEAN! MAYBE SAMMY! It looked like Jack Entratter was pulling out all the stops to fill the Copa Room.

When Jerry parked the car, we sat there for a few moments.

"What was your take on that, Jerry?" I asked. "Did he send those guys after me?"

"I'm gonna say yes, Mr. G.," Jerry said.

"Why?" I asked. "Why not whoever killed Susan Morrow?"

"I think if a killer had sent them after you, they woulda used their guns."

"Good point."

We got out of the car and headed for the door. I never even heard the first shot, and then Jerry was on me, dragging me to the ground, covering me with his body.

There were other people in the parking lot who started screaming and running. Jerry suddenly had his .45 in his right hand, but with his left he dragged me to cover behind a car.

"Jesus, what the hell—" I said.

"You hit, Mr. G.?" he asked.

"No, are you?"

"No."

"How many shots were there?" I asked.

"Three."

"Where are they?"

"I couldn't tell," Jerry said, "but I think they're gone."

We could hear someone crying, looked around the car and saw a woman on the ground, bleeding from the arm.

"Damn it!" I said. "Jerry, put your gun away and let's see what we can do."

He holstered his .45 and we rushed over to the woman to see how badly she was hurt. It turned out to be a scratch, but we made her stay on the ground and called an ambulance.

And, of course, someone called the cops . . .

***

Two officers responded along with the ambulance. We watched as they lifted the woman and placed her in the back, then I gave the attendant my card and said, "The Sands will foot the bill for her."

"Yes, Sir," he said. "I'll let them know."

I had also given the woman my card and told her she had a suite on the house when she got out of the hospital, if she wanted it. A man got into the ambulance with her, probably her husband, and he snapped, "That's the least you can do. This is crazy, havin' people get shot in your parkin' lot."

Quietly, I agreed with him.

***

"What the hell!" Jack Entratter exploded.

We stood in front of his desk, because he hadn't invited us to sit.

112

"Bullets flyin' in the parkin' lot, customers gettin' shot. What am I supposed to tell 'em?"

"Tell her it's all part of the 'mob owns Vegas' experience," I suggested.

He glared at me, and, for a moment, I thought his head was going to explode but then the redness in his face started to fade.

"That's not bad," he said. "Siddown, both of you."

We sat, as did he.

"What happened?" he asked, more calmly.

"Somebody took three shots at Mr. G.," Jerry said.

"Three?"

"Jerry saved my ass," I said. "He pulled me down before I even heard the first shot."

Entratter looked at Jerry.

"I guess I should thank you for that," he said.

"You don't gotta."

Entratter looked at me again.

"Did either of you see anybody?"

"No," I said. "And we don't know where the shots came from."

"Jerry," Entratter said, "no offense, but are you sure they were shootin' at Eddie?"

"Ain't nobody in Vegas got any reason to shoot at me, Mr. E.," Jerry said.

"So what's this about, Eddie? Hughes?"

"Could be." I told him about the three guys who tried to work me over, and then about going to talk with Maheu. "Jerry saved my bacon twice."

"So you get back from talkin' with Maheu and this happens," Entratter said. "Did Maheu have time to set it up?"

"He did if he put it in motion before we even talked," I said.

"And why would he do that?"

"Hughes found out I've been talkin' against 'im," I said. "He might've told Maheu to do somethin' about it."

"He told Maheu to have you killed?"

"He'd never admit to that," I said. "And he might not have. He might've only told Maheu to do something. Then Maheu made up his own mind."

"Okay," Entratter said, "I can see him havin' you worked over, but not killed. So that leaves us with the St. Jude thing for Danny, right?"

"Right," I said. "Somebody killed Susan Morrow, and now somebody tried to kill me."

"But why?"

"Maybe they think I'm gettin' close to findin' out who killed her."

"Are you?"

"Not a chance," I said. "I've got no clue."

"Okay," Entratter said, "I'm expectin' the police here, probably Hargrove, right?"

"Bet on it," I said.

"I'll handle him," he said. "And when the woman and her husband get back from the hospital, I want you kissin' their asses."

"I plan to," I said. "But Hargrove's gonna blow his stack if I'm not here."

"If I need you, I'll call you," Entratter said. "Right now, all we have is some nut firin' a gun in the parkin' lot and hittin' one of our customers. I'll keep you out of it if I can."

"I appreciate that, Jack," I said, as we stood up.

"He'd probably use this to toss you into a cell, and I need you on the streets. Frank wants you workin' with him against Hughes, and Danny's put a lot of faith in you."

"I see from the marquee you got Danny to add another show."

"Why not?" he asked. "He's here, ain't he? That's all."
Jerry and I left his office.

Chapter Thirty

After being shot at and yelled at, I needed a drink. But I didn't want to be in the casino or the hotel lobby if and when Detective Hargrove arrived, so I suggested we go to Jerry's suite.

"Beer or bourbon?" Jerry asked.

"Bourbon."

Jerry went behind the bar and produced a bottle of Jack Daniels. He poured me a healthy dose, then opened a bottle of Piels for himself. I sat at the bar and drank.

"You okay, Mr. G.?"

"I'm a little sore," I said, "and truth be told, still a bit shaky."

"That's natural," he said. "You ain't used to bein' shot at. And I had to yank you down pretty hard, so I'm sorry if I hurt ya."

"You saved my life, Jerry," I said. "There's nothin' to be sorry about."

"You want me to get ya a gun, Mr. G.?"

"No, I don't want a gun, Jerry," I said.

"I mean, if we're gonna keep pushn', somebody might get it into their head to shoot at ya, again."

"I get it, Jerry," I said. "But I don't need a gun. I'd probably shoot myself in the foot."

Jerry drank his Piels and opened another.

"Are you supposed to be drinkin' that much beer with your diabetes?" I asked.

"Believe it or not," he replied, "I ain't used ta bein' shot at, either."

Jerry left the bottle of Jack on the bar, so I poured myself another one.

"The shootin' has to be connected to the murder, not to Howard Hughes," I said. "It's the only thing that makes any sense."

"Agreed."

"I don't know what they think we're gettin' close to."

"Maybe nothin'," Jerry said. "Maybe they just want to keep us from even gettin' started."

"So, you're sayin' we're not close to anythin'."

"I don't see what it could be," Jerry said. "We ain't even found where the woman was stayin'."

"If we could find her room, that would be a start," I confirmed.

"You got the word out there," Jerry said. "What more can ya do?"

"I don't know," I said, "but there must be somethin'."

"Maybe the shamus is back from Tennessee with somethin'," Jerry suggested.

"Let's check."

There was a phone on the bar. I pulled it over and dialed Danny's office.

"Bardini Investigations," Penny answered.

"Penny, it's Eddie. Is Danny back in town?"

"He's on his way," she said. "His flight should be landing within the hour. I was gonna go and pick him up."

"We'll do it," I said. "Thanks."

"Eddie—" she started, but I hung up on her.

"She's really gonna be pissed at you, this time," Jerry said.

"I don't want her around if lead starts flyin' again." I drained my glass. "Let's go."

***

We managed to drive to the airport without getting shot at, again. There was a flight from Nashville landing in about twenty minutes.

"I just hope Danny gets off this plane with some information in his pocket," I said.

Chapter Thirty-One

"What're you guys doin' here?" Danny asked, when he saw us. "I thought Penny was pickin' me up."

"We called and told her we'd come and get you," I said. "Things have been happenin'."

"Well," Danny said, "let's get to the car and you can tell me what you've got, and I'll tell you what I've got."

"Let's just keep our eyes open in the parking lot," I said.

"Why?"

"I'll tell you while we walk."

***

"Now you're makin' me wish I'd taken my gun with me," Danny said, when we reached the car.

"You went to Nashville without a gun?" Jerry asked.

"I was only gonna look for information, Big Guy," Danny said, "not a firefight."

"We didn't have to go lookin'," I said. "They found us."

We got into the car, with Jerry behind the wheel and Danny in the backseat.

"So you think the shootin' was because of this murder?" Danny asked.

"I can't see why else," I said. "The only other thing we're workin' on is Howard Hughes, and I don't think he wants to kill me. He's a businessman."

"Well," Danny said, glacing behind us, "it doesn't look like any-one's on our tail. Wanna take me to my office, Big Guy?"

"You got it, Gumshoe."

"What'd you find out, Danny?" I asked.

"I looked into all three of Danny Thomas' St. Jude people," Danny said. "None of them have any kind of police record, none of them are deep in debt, one of them—Clarence Foster—plays in a weekly poker game."

"So he's a gambler."

"If you call a quarter-and-a-half gamblin', then yes," Danny said.

"Morrow and Dominguez, no indication that they gamble?" I asked.

"No."

"And Dominguez and Foster, are they in Nashville?"

"They were when I got there, and still there when I left."

"So only Susan came to Vegas."

"Looks like it."

Jerry pulled onto Fremont Street.

"We'll drop you off and keep goin'," I said. "I don't want whoever shot at us to target you."

"Don't worry," Danny said, "I'll be carryin' from now on."

Jerry pulled up in front of Danny's office and let him out.

"Penny's gonna be kind of pissed at me," I said. "Maybe you can smooth things over."

"Sure," he said. "Then I'll do a report for my files. I'll send you a copy."

"That'd be great, Danny," I said. "Thanks."

"Let me know if you guys need any more help."

"We owe you a big meal."

"I'll collect real soon," he said, and went to his office door.

"Where to, Mr. G.?"

For want of anywhere else I said, "Let's take a ride to the police impound lot. Maybe we can get a look at the car Susan Morrow was drivin'."

"You think you'll find somethin' the cops didn't?" Jerry asked.

"You never know," I said.

"You wanna tell me where it is?"

"Just drive," I said, "I'll give you directions."

***

The impound lot was manned by civilians, not cops. That would make it easier to get in. I had several ways I could go, offer the impound guy money, tickets to a show, or a credit line at the Sands.

"Really?" Jerry asked, as he drove my Caddy. "A line of credit?"

"If he's a gambler, he'd go for it," I said.

"Gambler or not," Jerry said, "he'd take it."

"Or go for cash."

"There's that," Jerry agreed. "Whataya wanna try first?"

"Why don't we just ask?"

***

Rather than being located downtown, the police department impound lot was outside the city, on the edge of the desert. Jerry parked the Caddy just outside the gate. As we approached on foot, a civilian stepped out of a phone booth-size guard shack. He was six feet tall, in his thirties, wearing work clothes, wiping his hands with a red, greasy rag.

"Can I help you?"

"A car was brought in here recently. A woman was murdered in it."

"Only one car like that lately," the man said. "A two-year-old Ke-nosha Cadillac."

The Nash Rambler was also known as the "Kenosha Cadillac," be-cause they were manufactured in Kenosha, Wisconsin.

"What's on your mind?" the man asked.

"I'd like to take a look at the car," I said.

The man examined me, and then Jerry.

"You ain't cops."

"Hell, no, we ain't," Jerry agreed.

"What's in it for me?"

"What do you want?" I asked. "Anythin' other than cash?"

"Cash'll do it," the man said.

"How much?"

The man smiled, stuck the dirty red rag into his back pocket, then folded his arms across his chest.

"Make me an offer."

Instead, I just took out a hundred-dollar bill from my pocket and handed it to him. He accepted it and put it in his pocket.

"I usually go and get some dinner about now," he said. "I should be back in about an hour."

"Good to know," I said.

He walked to a four or five-year-old Chrysler parked nearby, got in and drove away.

I tried the front gate, found it unlocked.

"After you," I said to Jerry.

Chapter Thirty-Two

We found only one Rambler on the grounds. The rental papers, still in the glove compartment, identified the renter as Susan Morrow.

"Got it!" I said, from behind the wheel. I took the keys from the ignition and held them out to Jerry. "Check the trunk, will you, Jerry?"

"Sure thing, Mr. G.," he said, snatching the keys from my hand.

Jerry opened the trunk and began rummaging around, while I checked the front and back seats, the visor and the glove compartment.

"Nothin' back here but a spare tire and jack, Mr. G.," Jerry called out.

"I've got somethin'," I called back.

He closed the trunk and joined me. I showed him the card I had just gotten from the driver's side visor.

"What is it?" Jerry asked.

"A visitor's pass for the Sunrise Gym."

"If she was in Vegas to gamble, what was she doin' at a gym?"

"That's what we have to go and find out," I said, pocketing the pass. "Let's put this car back the way we found it."

I had made sure the maps I'd found of L.A. and Vegas went back into the glove compartment, and the visors were up. By the time the attendant returned we were back outside the gate.

"All done?" he asked.

"Yes, thank you," I said.

"For what? I didn't do anythin'."

"Right," I said.

We went back to the Caddy.

"Sunrise Gym?" Jerry asked as he got behind the wheel.

"Yep," I said. "I'll direct you."

***

The Sunrise Gym was on Flamingo Road, a few blocks off the strip. We parked in the parking lot among some snazzy sports cars, and some station wagons. The clientele of a gym like Sunrise was made up of showgirls trying to stay in shape, housewives and husbands fighting off the extra pounds, lifeguards, dealers, waitresses, all trying to keep in shape for their jobs. There'd even be some businessmen and women trying to make sure they looked good in their suits.

We stopped at the front desk and showed a girl wearing a workout leotard the guest pass.

"Yes, we very often give these out to people who don't live here, just visiting."

"Do you remember this girl?" I asked, describing Susan Morrow.

"I'm sorry, no," the girl said. "That sounds like a lot of women who come in here."

"Do you think there'd be anyone else who might remember her?"

"You could ask, but it might be easier if I just look up the name of the member who made her a guest."

"You can do that?"

"Sure," she said with a smile, but then her face clouded. "But maybe I shouldn't be talkin' about our members."

"Doll," I said, "do you like to gamble? Watch shows?"

"Well, sure, who doesn't?"

"My name's Eddie Gianelli. I work at the Sands." I gave her my card. "Any time you want to come in and have a good time, you give me a call. I'll see to it you have a ball."

"Wow," she said, holding my card in one hand, but looking at Jerry. "You work at the Sands?"

"Sure he does," I said, quickly.

"So you can look up that member's name?" I pushed.

"There's a member number on the pass. Take me a sec." She had been tossing glances at Jerry the whole time, and now she looked right at him. "Maybe you wanna come into the back and help me, Big Guy?"

"Huh? Uh, no," Jerry said, "I don't think so."

"Oh." She seemed disappointed. "Okay. I'll be right back."

As she turned and left, I asked Jerry, "Why didn't you go with her?"

"Not my type, he said.

"What the hell's wrong with 'er?"

He made a face.

"Too athletic," he said.

A few moments later the girl returned, brandishing a three-by-five index card.

"I got it," she said.

"Can you write it down for us, doll?" I asked.

She grabbed a message pad from near the phone and jotted the name and info down. I accepted it and looked at the name.

"Lisa Delacorte," I read out loud. "And what's your name?"

"Gwen," she said, "Gwen Taylor."

"Gwen, do you know Lisa? Or anything about her?"

"She comes in three times a week, like clockwork. She doesn't try to bulk up, just maintain her figure, which is pretty good."

"As good as yours?"

Gwen had a dancer's body, long and lean. I was willing to bet she was waiting for a slot to open up on a line, somewhere.

"Better," she said.

"Is she here now?"

"No, today's not one of her days."

"And where does she work? Do you know?"

125

"One of the casinos," she said. "I'm not sure which, but they have a topless show."

I could've figured that out, but we had her home address.

"Gwen, thanks a lot," I said. "Don't forget to call me if you want to come in."

"Oh, I will, Mr. Gianelli." She looked at Jerry. " 'bye."

"Yeah," Jerry said, "good-bye."

"She likes you," I said, on the way out. "You're passin' up a sure thing."

"I don't like workout broads," he grumbled.

Chapter Thirty-Three

Lisa Delacorte lived in a highrise on West Sahara Avenue. We parked on the street out front and went inside. It was a building with a doorman standing behind a desk.

"You guys are gonna get a ticket out there," he said.

"We're not gonna be here that long," I said. "We're lookin' for Lisa Delacorte."

"She's on six," the doorman said. "She shares it with two other girls." He was in his forties, looked us up and down with knowing eyes. "You guys ain't cops."

"No," I said, "my name's Eddie Gianelli, this is Jerry. We work at the Sands."

"The Sands. Hey, that's a pretty cool place. Rat Pack, right?"

"Well," I said, "Frank likes to call 'em the Summit."

"You know Sinatra?" he asked.

"I know them all, friend," I said. "But right now, we need to see Miss Delacorte. Is she home?"

"Yep," he said, "but I can't let you up."

"Why not?"

"It's my job to keep these girls safe."

"We're not tryin' to sneak up on her," I said. "Call her and tell 'em we're here to see her about a friend of hers."

He gave me a look.

"You really know Frank and Dean?" he asked.

"He does," Jerry said, speaking for the first time. "He's good friends with 'em."

"Look," he said, "I got a girlfriend who loves those guys—"

"Say no more," I said. "Next show you've got free tickets."

"A show and dinner?" he asked.

"And dinner."

"Hang on."

He picked up the phone and dialed.

"Miss Delacorte? This is Vincent. There's two gents down here to see you. They're from the Sands. I don't know. I'll ask." He covered the phone with his hand. "She wants to know what it's about?"

"Tell her Susan Morrow."

"They say it's about Susan Morrow. Yes, Ma'am, right away." He hung up. "She says to send you right up. Six-oh-five."

"Thanks, Vincent."

"No, thank you," he said. "In advance. I'll unlock the elevator."

In the elevator I said to Jerry, "One thing bothers me."

"What's that?"

"Why was the gym card still in the visor?" I asked. "Why didn't the cops find it? Why didn't Hargrove find it?"

"Maybe because he's an asshole who doesn't know his job?" Jerry asked.

"Actually," I said, "he is an asshole, but I do think he kinda knows his job. I can't believe he just missed it."

"So you think he left it there on purpose?" Jerry asked.

"Why would he do that?"

"Because he wanted somebody else to find it?" he offered.

"I don't know," I said. "Could he have wanted me to find it?"

"How would he know you'd search the car?"

As the doors opened, I said, "We did get into that car lot pretty easy."

"Maybe," Jerry said, "he wants you to do his job for him, Mr. G."

"I don't know," I said, again. "We've gotta think about this some more, after we talk to Miss Delacorte."

When we got to six-oh-five, I rang the buzzer. It was immediately opened by a pretty brunette, wearing jeans and a t-shirt. She looked harried and a bit unkempt.

"Lisa?" I asked.

"No," she said, "I'm one of her roommates, Jennifer. And I'm on my way out. This is about her friend, Susan?"

"Yeah, but—"

"I hope you got good news for her," she said, "because the girl's a basket case. I'm sorry, I've got to go. She's inside." She hurried off toward the elevator, leaving the door open.

I knocked on the wide-open door.

"Lisa? Hello?"

When there was no answer, we walked in. As we got deeper into the apartment, we found a blonde girl standing in the living room, looking panicked and holding a gun in both hands, pointing it right at us.

"Who the hell are you?" she demanded. "Where's Susan?"

Chapter Thirty-Four

"Take it easy, Lisa," I said, holding my hands out to her. I was showing her they were empty and warding off a bullet. Jerry stood very still behind me.

"Who are you?" she asked.

"Like Vincent told you," I said. "I'm Eddie Gianelli from the Sands. This is my colleague, Jerry."

"That thirty-eight don't take much pull on the trigger," Jerry said. "Be careful."

"Eddie Gianelli?" she said. "Eddie G., from the Sands?"

"That's right."

"I've heard of you," she said. "I work at the Stardust." Then she frowned. "Can you prove it?"

"Yeah, sure." I dug my wallet out. "Here's my driver's license." I held it out to her.

She reached with her left hand, grabbed it and looked at it. Then she dropped her arms to her side and practically fell onto the sofa.

"Oh my God," she said, "I'm so sorry. I've just been so worried about Susan, since she disappeared."

I looked at Jerry, who stepped forward and reached for her gun.

"Can I have that?" he asked.

"Oh, yeah, sure," she said, giving it up.

Jerry stuck the gun—which looked like a toy in his big hand—in his jacket pocket.

"You mind if we sit?" I asked, and she waved a hand.

I was wondering when to broach the subject of Susan being dead. Right now, she was upset only that her friend was missing.

"When's the last time you saw Susan?" I asked.

"It's been . . . days. She showed up last week, saying she needed a place to stay. She was all upset, and I thought she was having man trouble. But then I realized it was worse than that. She was really scared,"

Susan hadn't seemed scared when she came to see me. That was still puzzling. What was that visit all about? Was she just looking for a place to spend the night? But it wasn't a coincidence. She had my name in her purse.

"And she didn't tell you why?"

"No. Then one day she went out and . . . never came back. I've been calling and calling her at home, but there's no answer."

"What about the police?"

"I called them," she said. "They're no help. They say I can't report her missing because I'm not a family member. And there's nothing suspicious about her disappearance. They say she's an adult and can come and go as she pleases."

This sounded like a case of the left hand not knowing what the right hand was doing. Missing Persons hadn't connected this missing person with Hargrove's body.

"Did you tell them her name?" I asked.

"I didn't get that far on the phone," she said. "As soon as they heard I wasn't a family member, they rushed me off."

"What's with the gun?" Jerry asked.

"I just have that for protection," she said. "Even three girls living together need protection, right? My old boyfriend got it for me."

"Why point it at us?" Jerry asked.

"I just thought . . . I don't know. I panicked after I told Vincent to send you up. I told Jennifer she better get out. She had stuff to do anyway."

"And where's your other roommate?" I asked.

"Carol's at work," she said. "We all work at different casinos. Jen and I are in shows, and Carol's a waitress."

Lisa was in her twenties, tall and stacked, just the kind of girl you'd like to see in a topless show. She was dressed as her friend Jennifer had been—t-shirt and jeans—and the shirt was being tested. Her hair and makeup were more expertly done.

"So Susan didn't mention any names," I said.

"No," she said, glumly. Then she looked at us and asked the question I was waiting for.

"Wait. Why are you asking about her? And why are you here? How did you know—"

"Lisa," I said, "I'm sorry, but . . . Susan's dead."

Her eyes went wide and immediately filled with tears. You couldn't fake her reaction.

"W-what?"

"She was found in her car a couple of days ago," I said. "Somebody killed her."

"Oh my God." She covered her mouth with both hands. "She was so scared!"

Jerry looked around, saw a box of tissues on a small table, grabbed it and gave it to her. She immediately yanked out two and held them to her face.

"B-but . . . what're you doing here?"

"We found her guest gym card in the visor of her rental car," I said. "We went to the gym, and they gave us your address."

"B-but, you're not the police."

"I know," I said, "we were looking for Susan on a whole different matter. I don't think it had anything to do with her being scared."

"Why?" she said. "Why do you—did you want her?"

"It has to do with St. Jude," I said.

"Oh, that charity she worked for?"

"Yes," I said, "and I might as well ask you . . . look, Danny Thomas believes somebody's been skimming money from the organization."

"Skimming?" she repeated.

"Stealin'," Jerry said.

Her eyes went wide.

"Susan would *never* steal from St. Jude!" she cried. "She loves that place!"

"That's what I was gonna ask you," I said. "We've been tryin' to determine if her murder had anything to do with St. Jude."

"Oh God," she said, "this—this is horrible."

"Lisa, I'm sorry, but did Susan leave anything here? A suitcase? An overnight bag?"

"Yes, it's in my bedroom. I—I'll get it."

She got up, left the room and came back moments later with a small, pink overnight bag. She sat back down and placed it on the sofa next to her.

"She said she packed in a hurry," she said. "I was actually letting her borrow some of my clothes."

From my time with Susan, it occurred to me that Lisa's clothes would be a little too big on her.

I leaned over and opened the bag, rifled through quickly. She was right! Susan had packed in a hurry. There wasn't much in there, certainly nothing helpful. When I pulled my hand out, it smelled of Susan's perfume, which I remembered from my night with her.

"Lisa, was Susan a gambler?"

"Hell, no," Lisa said. "She came here every once in a while to see shows and party, that's all."

"Okay, one more question and then we'll leave you alone," I said. "Did Susan ever mention my name?"

"No, I don't think so," she said. "I mean, I've heard your name around the casino, so if she'd mentioned it, I would've recognized it."

"Right," I said, "okay. Look, this has been a shock. Will you be all right?"

"I—I suppose so," she said.

"Can we call anybody for you?"

"N-no." she said. "I can call one of the girls. When they hear what happened, they'll come home. They both met Susan and kinda liked her."

"All right, then." Jerry and I stood. "I'm sorry we had to bring you this news."

"W-will I have to talk to the police?"

"I'm sure you will, at some point."

Suddenly, she got angry.

"Well, if I do, I'm gonna give them a piece of my mind!" she growled. "Maybe if they'd taken my report that she was missing days ago, she'd still be alive."

Chapter Thirty-Five

"Did you believe 'er?" Jerry asked me in the elevator.

"Totally," I said.

"Even when she thought to ask for her gun back on our way to the door?"

"Well," I pointed out, "she's lookin' to protect herself even more, now."

We waved at Vincent on the way out and made our way to the Caddy.

"Well, what now?" he asked.

I leaned against the car with my butt. Jerry did the same with his hip.

"We know a few things we didn't know before," I said. "We know where she was stayin', we know she was afraid of somebody."

"But why'd she come to Vegas?" Jerry asked.

"Could be she just needed a place to hide, and thought of her friend, Lisa. That was why she flew to L.A. first, and then drove here, to get to whoever she was afraid of off her back."

"But why'd she come and see you?" Jerry said. "If it wasn't about St. Jude, then it's a coincidence that both her and Danny Thomas came to see you?"

"Yes," I said, "coincidence."

"So we're no closer to findin' out who's stealin' St. Jude's money."

"Or who killed Susan Morrow."

"So what now?" Jerry asked. "Are you gonna tell Hargrove about Lisa?"

"I suppose we should," I said. "He's workin' on the murder and needs to know everything. But . . ."

". . . but it's funny to think about him stumbling around in the dark."

"True," I said, laughing, "but the murder does have to be solved. I'm still wondering about this gym pass, though."

"You don't think Hargrove just missed it?" Jerry asked.

"I guess it's possible he's just that slipshod at his work," I said

"Maybe," Jerry said, "he had somebody else search the car."

"Yes," I said, "someone else who was inept." I took the card from my pocket. "Maybe we should send it to Hargrove anonymously."

"That girl at the gym, she'll tell 'im we were there."

"We might be able to get her to keep quiet." I put the card back in my pocket. "Well, let's give it some thought."

We got into the car, and he started the engine.

"Where to?"

"Back to the Sands," I said. "Let's get something to eat."

"I'm for that."

***

When we got back, I checked for messages. There were none. We went to the Garden Room and ordered some dinner. The waitress we had was one of the senior teams who wasn't impressed with Jerry, me or anyone else. All she did was bring our food.

"Fries?" I said to him, looking at his plate.

"Don't gimme a hard time," he said. "I'm hungry."

I reached out, grabbed a bunch of fries from his plate and dropped them onto mine.

"Hey!" he complained.

"Just tryin' to help my diabetic friend stay alive," I said.

"Fuckin' diabetes is a pain in my ass," he grumbled.

"Let's talk about somethin' else, then," I proposed.

Before we could start, though, one of the bellboys from the hotel came in and approached our table.

"Hey, Pete, what's up?" I asked.

"A message just came in for you, Mr. G.," Pete said.

He was in his twenties— he had been a bellboy at the Sands for a couple of years. I wondered if all the employees were going to keep their jobs under the new owner, Hughes?

"Thanks, Pete." I tipped him.

"Thanks, Mr. G.," he said and hurried off.

"Who's it from?" Jerry asked.

I unfolded it and read.

"Dino," I said.

"What's he say?"

"He wants me to meet him at the golf course tomorrow mornin'," I said, handing him the paper.

"And be dressed to play,'" Jerry read. "You don't play golf, do ya, Mr. G.?"

"Not really," I said. "I mean, I've swung a club a time or two, but that's it."

He handed the message back and returned to his meal.

"Whataya think this is about?"

"I dunno." I pocketed the paper and picked up my fork. "I guess I'll find out tomorrow."

***

I arrived at the Stardust Country Club bright and early, dressed for golf. I didn't have any of those weird plaid pants lots of golfers wear, so I wore white and a light blue shirt.

Dino was sitting at the bar, drinking orange juice. I know everyone else in the room thought it was a screwdriver, but I knew him. I knew he drank apple juice on stage, so he was drinking pure orange juice this morning.

Dean saw me coming and smiled. He was wearing golf shoes, black-and-white plaid golf pants, a yellow cardigan over a light blue button-down shirt.

"What are you wearin'?" he asked.

"The closest thing I have to golf clothes," I said.

"Orange juice?"

"Sure."

He waved at the bartender, who set one up for me. I hadn't eaten breakfast. The juice was cold and refreshing.

"What's goin' on?" I asked.

"We've got a sextet today," he said. "You, me, Frank, and three casino owners. We're gonna convince them not to sell to Hughes. And we'll show 'em a good time, while we're at it."

"You know I don't play golf, right?"

"Don't worry, Pally," he said. "All you've gotta do is hit the little white ball. Frank and I will take care of the rest."

"Frank agreed to this?"

"Sure," Dino said. "Here he comes."

I turned and looked. Frank had white golf shoes, yellow plaid pants and a red-collared shirt.

"What are you drinkin'?" he asked us.

"Orange juice," I said.

The bartender looked at Frank. Like the waitress Jerry and I had the night before, this fella had worked there long enough not to be impressed by anybody.

"I'll have what they're havin'," Frank said, "only put some life in mine."

"Got it," the bartender said.

He poured Frank a glass of juice, added Vodka and handed it to him.

"Thanks," Frank said, and sipped gratefully.

"Who's comin'?" Frank asked Dino.

Dean told him three names from three of the biggest casinos.

"I spoke to a couple of 'em, already," I said.

"That's okay," Dean said. "We're gonna reinforce whatever you said to them."

"Yeah," Frank said, "we're gonna make damn sure they don't sell to that sonofabitch."

"Now, no threats, Frank," Dino said. "We're just gonna convince 'em."

"Of course," Frank said, with a smile, "no threats."

Chapter Thirty-Six

We played a full eighteen holes.

Well, I should say Dean shot eighteen holes. I flailed away at the ball, hitting it into sand traps and woods almost every time. Frank did better, even though he was concentrating more on talking with the three casino guys. By the eighteenth hole they were all swearing they wouldn't even be talking with Howard Hughes.

Later, Dean, Frank and I went back to the clubhouse while the casino execs got dressed and left.

"Whataya think?" Frank asked us.

"I think you were very firm, Frank," Dean said. "I also think I shot one of my best games." He looked at me. "I think you shot your weight, Pally."

"I never claimed to be a golfer." I looked at Frank. "But I think you got the point across, Frank."

"Yeah, well," Frank said, "Hughes is still sittin' on a mountain of cash. I'm thinkin' it's all gonna depend on how he wants to use it."

"I guess we'll just have to wait and see," I said.

Dino drank his apple juice, while Frank worked on his bourbon. It was way past screwdriver time. I had a beer.

Frank swiveled around on his bar stool, slapped me on the back and said, "What's on your agenda, Clyde?"

"I'm still workin' on a job for Danny Thomas."

Frank looked past me at Dean and said, "Hey, he was pretty good the other night. The old Lebanese schnoz has still got it, huh?"

"What old?" Dean asked. "He's three years older than you, Frank."

Frank touched his face and said, "Yeah, but you gotta admit, he looks older."

Dean started to laugh. "You guys remember when we crashed his act in nineteen-sixty?"

"We didn't crash it," Frank said. "He called us up on stage."

Dean gave me a serious look. "Is this about that St. Jude thing?"

"He told you about that?"

"Come on, Pally," Frank said. "Who do you think told him to contact you?"

"He didn't tell us much," Dino said. "Just that somebody was stealin' from the charity fund."

"We figured that anybody grabbin' that kind of cash might be gamblin' it. I mean, why else would somebody want that much money?"

"Buy a car? A house?"

"Gamblin'," Dino said, nodding. "The root of all evil."

"I thought that was liquor," Frank said.

"Liquor is quicker," Dean said, and they raised their glasses to each other.

"I don't know about the logic of that," I said. "If it wasn't for the murder—"

"Whoa," Frank said, "murder?"

"Okay," Dino said, "come on, give."

So I told them about Susan Morrow's murder, and how I couldn't even be sure if it was connected to the St. Jude business or not.

"How are you gonna find that out, Eddie?" Frank asked.

"Danny, Jerry and I are askin' around," I said. "That much money can't stay hidden forever."

"Well," Dino said, "I hope we're right and it's here in Vegas, with whoever stole it. If it is, you'll find it, Eddie." He looked at Frank. "Another nine holes?"

"Why not?"

"So how much per stroke?" Frank asked.

"I told you gambling was the root of all evil," Dean said. "It's a bet."

I left without finding out how much they were playing per stroke.

***

When I got back to the Sands, the desk clerk waved me over frantically.

"I got a message for you, Eddie," he said, "from your buddy, Jerry."

"What is it?"

The kid started shuffling pieces of paper.

"It's here somewhere . . ."

"Just tell me!"

He snapped to.

"He said that girl . . . the one you guys talked to yesterday . . . called, all in a panic. She said she needed help."

"And he went alone?"

"Um, well, yeah."

And I had the Caddy.

"How did he go?"

"He took one of our cars."

The Sands kept cars in the parking lot for employees to use.

"How long ago was this?"

"I'd say . . . about an hour."

I ran out the front door.

Chapter Thirty-Seven

When I rushed into the lobby, the apartment house doorman, Vincent, saw me and jumped out from behind the desk, holding his hands out to stop me.

"Whoa, whoa, they ain't up there!"

"Where are they?"

"The cops took 'em all away."

"All?"

"Miss Delacorte, your guy, and the two other guys."

"Were they okay?"

"Miss Delacorte was kinda bruised," he said. "The big guy was okay, but the other two, he smoked 'em."

"Who called the cops?" I asked.

"Musta been some other guest on the floor who heard the ruckus."

Great. One way or another, Hargrove was going to hear about this. Jerry was going to be in trouble. I could've called one of the lawyers who worked for the Sands, but instead I called Kaminsky. He was a lawyer I had used a time or two.

"He could end up at the detention center?" Kaminsky said. "You want to meet me there?"

"We're involved in something Kaminsky."

"Why doesn't that surprise me?"

"He's gonna be in Hargrove's office. I know it!"

"Okay, then let's meet there."

We hung up.

***

When I entered the building, Kaminsky, a small, Jewish gent with an attaché case was waiting.

"You were right," he said. "Patrol picked him up, but Hargrove jumped in pretty quick. He's got him in an interrogation room."

"Have you seen him, yet?"

"No," Kaminsky said. "Jerry killed two guys."

"And may have saved a girl's life!" I reminded him. "What's he told Hargrove?"

"Nothing," Kaminsky said. "Hargrove says Jerry's waiting for you."

"All right," I said, "let's you and me go and see 'im."

"Okay, but get this," Kaminsky said, handing me a dollar. "You work for me. Got it?"

"I got it."

Hargrove bitched and moaned as usual, but he also gloated.

"I've got your big buddy this time, Eddie," he told me. "Got 'im good."

He let Kaminsky and me in to see Jerry, who told me what had happened . . .

***

Jerry's story

When Lisa called the Sands and couldn't get you, Mr. G., that kid at the desk got ahold of me.

"Whatasamatta, Lisa?" I asked.

"Is this Eddie?"

"It's Jerry. I was with Eddie—"

"There's two more men on the way up here," Lisa said, sounding panicked. "I told them not to come, but they said it was about the money."

"They said 'the' money?" I asked.

"Y-yes," she said. "I-I don't know what money they're talking about."

"Lock the doors," I told her, "I'm on my way. And if you have to use that gun, do it."

"Oh God!" she said, but I dropped the phone.

"I need a car," I said to the desk clerk.

"Um, the valets have keys to the Sands cars."

I ran outside. Mr. G., you know I've got to be pretty good friends with some of the valets, so I talked to one and he gave me a car pretty quick. I drove back over to Lisa's apartment and ran into the lobby."

"What's goin' on?" the doorman asked me.

"Did you let two men go up to Lisa's apartment?"

"Well, yeah," he answered, "they said they was from the Sands. I thought they was your people—"

"I gotta get up there fast. Can you run the elevator on express?"

"Yeah, sure," he said, "come on."

We got into one of the elevators and he stuck a key in and ran it right up to Lisa's floor. When the door opened, I ran down the hall. Her door was wide open. It had been kicked in, Mr. G. I went inside and she was wrestling; with two jokers. I think they may have been two of the same ones that jumped you in the parking lot.

They had her down on the floor, so I yelled, Get offa her! They turned and looked at me. I didn't see them go for their guns. I think maybe the gun one of 'em used was Lisa's. Anyway, they turned and started shootin', so I pulled my piece and started firin' back . . .

***

"I acted on my instincts, Mr. G.," Jerry finished. "You know, when somebody starts shootin' at me . . ."

". . . you shoot back," I said. "I get it." I looked at Kaminsky. "Self-defense."

Kaminsky slapped me on the back and said, "I'll get him out." He got up and left the room.

"How's Lisa?" I asked.

"Bruised," he said. "They took her to the hospital."

"Do you know what she's gonna tell 'em?"

"I told her not to mention Susan, Mr. G.," Jerry said. "I knew if Hargrove connected the two, we'd be here all night."

"Good man," I said. "We'll talk to her when we get out of here."

"You think I'm gettin' out?" he asked.

"I think so," I said, "but not your forty-five."

"Shit!" he swore.

***

We wanted to get Lisa out of the hospital, but the cops got to her first. I convinced Kaminsky to represent her. A couple of hours later, the bandy-legged little lawyer came out of the building with Jerry on one side and Lisa on the other.

"Are you all right?" I asked her.

"I'm fine," she said, "thanks to all of you. Especially Jerry. I thought they were gonna kill me!"

"All right," I said, "we'll take you home."

"I can't go home yet," she said.

"Fine, we'll go someplace and talk." I turned to Kaminsky, thanked him and shook hands. Then he shook hands with Jerry and got a hug from Lisa before heading off.

We got into the Caddy with Lisa and headed for the Sands. Sometime the next day I'd send somebody to pick up the car Jerry had used.

We took Lisa to the Sands, into the Garden Room and got us all some coffee.

"What happened?" I asked her.

"That's what I was gonna ask you!" she said. "They came bursting in and demanding the money. What money?"

I looked at Jerry. It seemed fairly obvious that these men thought Susan Morrow had the St. Jude money. Maybe they killed her before they could get her to talk, so they decided to go after her friends.

"Where are Carol and Jennifer?" I asked.

"They went out for the night."

"We have to keep them from going home," I said to Jerry.

"B-but . . . those men are dead . . . aren't they?" Lisa asked.

"Those two are," I said, "but there's at least one more."

"How do you know?"

"Those two and one other attacked me in the parking lot outside," I said. "Jerry saved my ass, just like he saved yours, only without the shots."

"But what happens if they go home and someone's there?" she asked.

"We have to get there first," I said.

"Can I stay here?" she asked.

"Will Jennifer remember me?" I asked. We had run into her coming out of the apartment, but only for a moment.

"Oh, yes," Lisa said, "she thought you were a very handsome man."

"Okay," I said, "I'm gonna get somebody to take you to a room while Jerry and I go and get your girlfriends. The three of you can stay here until it's all over."

"I have one more question," she said.

"Shoot," I said.

She waved her arms frantically.

"Until what's over?"

Chapter Thirty-Eight

I got one of the desk clerks to give her a room, and a bellboy to take her up there.

"Don't come down, don't open the door for anyone but us," I instructed her. "We'll be back as soon as we can."

"I'm still totally confused," she said, "but okay."

With that taken care of we jumped in the Caddy and drove to her building, again.

"Is Miss Delacorte all right?" the doorman asked as we came in.

"She's fine," I said. "She's gonna be staying somewhere else for a while, until it's safe to come back."

"Well, good for her," he said, "but am I in danger?"

"No," I said. "Are her roommates up there?"

"They came back about half-an-hour ago. I had to tell them that their door was broken down, there was a shooting . . . the works."

"And they stayed in the apartment?"

"They're waiting to hear from Lisa."

"Give 'em a call," I said, "tell 'em we're here and if they want to check that we're legit, they can call the Sands and talk to Lisa."

I wrote the number down for him and he called upstairs. I heard him speak to Jennifer, and then hang up.

"She's gonna call Lisa and call back."

It only took a few minutes for his phone to ring.

"You can go up," he said. "Please tell the girls I'm still trying to get maintenance to come and fix their door."

"We will."

When we got to the floor, Jennifer, the pretty, slightly disheveled brunette, was waiting at the open doorway.

"Eddie G., right?" she asked.

"That's right," I said. "This is Jerry."

"You saved Lisa."

Jerry nodded.

"Come on in."

As we entered, we saw a slightly chubby, but pretty blonde sitting on the sofa.

"This is Carol," Jennifer said. "Can you tell us what's going on?"

"Yes," I said, "but not here. We'll take you to Lisa, where the three of you will be safe, and then we can talk. It'll be easier to explain when we're all together."

Carol stood up, wringing her hands, and said, "Then let's go. I've been a nervous wreck since we got back."

***

We drove both girls to the Sands, Jerry following me in the car he'd taken from our carpool. When Lisa opened the door to her suite, the three girls hugged tightly. Jerry and I gave them a few moments before breaking it up.

"You girls are gonna have to stay here for a little while," I said.

"How long?" Jennifer asked. "We have jobs!"

"What's goin on?" Carol demanded.

"Sit down, and we'll try to explain."

The three girls sat down together on the sofa. Jerry and I stood in front of them.

"Apparently," I said, "somebody believes that Susan Morrow stole money from the St. Jude's Children's Research Hospital."

"What?" Jennifer said.

"Susan would never—" Lisa started, but I cut her off.

"At this point, it doesn't matter whether she actually did steal it, or didn't, somebody thinks she did. I believe that's why they killed her, why they attacked me and warned me off, and attacked you today."

"But you don't think she did it," Lisa said.

"That's what I'm tryin' to find out," I said. "Who took the money, who killed Susan, and who's after you because they think you know where the money is." I paused for effect, then asked, "Do you?"

"Wha—no!" Lisa said. "None of us knows anything about any money. I can't believe Susan would do that."

"But did you really know her that well?" Carol asked.

"Yes, I did!" Lisa snapped. "She's—she was my friend."

"Look," I said, "right now it doesn't matter if she did or not. Somebody thinks she did, and they think you knew about it."

"What about the police?" Carol demanded. "Where are they in all this?"

"The police are working on Susan's murder."

She looked at her girlfriends. "Why are we here with these two? They're not the police." She looked at me. "I want the police."

"You're free to go to the cops, Carol," I said. "Any of you can go."

"But you wouldn't," Lisa said.

"No," I said.

"Why not?" Jennifer asked.

"I know the detective who's been assigned," I said, "and quite frankly, he's an idiot."

"I don't care," Carol said, stamping her foot. "I want cops, not these guys." She looked at me. "Who are you, anyway?"

"Carol, sit down!" Lisa snapped.

Carol's mouth snapped shut and she sat, but she didn't look happy.

"These men saved my life," Lisa said. "I'm going along with them. Jen?"

Jennifer looked around at the suite they were in.

"We're gonna stay here?" she asked.

"That's right," I said.

"For free?"

"Yes."

"And what about clothes?"

"We can have somebody go to your place and pick some up," I said, "or just buy you new ones."

Jennifer looked at Carol.

"I'm with Lisa," she said.

"You're both crazy," Carol said.

Lisa stood up and walked over to me.

"We'll talk to her," she said, keeping her voice down. "She'll come around."

"I hope so," I said. "If she wants to go, we can't keep her here by force."

"I understand," Lisa said.

She walked us to the door.

"I'll have someone come up," I said, "get your sizes, and then go out and buy some things. It won't be anything fancy, just so you can get through the next few days. Hopefully, everything will be over by then."

"Thank you, Eddie," Lisa said, "I owe you—especially you, ya big lug." She gave Jerry a hug. "When this is over, you and me are gonna do somethin'."

Jerry looked embarrassed, and we left the suite.

"She's a nice broad, Mr. G.," he said, in the hall.

"I know, Jerry."

"What the hell do I know about bein' with a nice broad?"

Chapter Thirty-Nine

"Now whatta we do?" Jerry asked when we got to the hotel lobby. "How long can we keep those girls here?"

"You, know," I said. "Danny's still here. I think I should talk to him."

"What are ya gonna tell Mr. Thomas?"

"Well, it looks to me like Susan might actually have stolen the money."

"And who do you think those guys were?"

"She may have had a partner or partners, and maybe she took off with the money and they're tryin' to find it."

"After killin' her?"

"That was probably a mistake," I said. "I mean, why kill her before you have the money?"

"So they figured one of her girlfriends would know where the money is."

"That answers your first question," I said. "We have to keep them here until we find the money."

"How you wanna play it?"

"I'll go up and brief Danny on what we think, and you wait here for Penny. When she gets here, take her up and introduce her to the girls."

"What if the shamus comes with 'er?" Jerry asked.

"Believe me," I said, "Penny's not gonna bring Danny to meet three showgirls."

"What about the cops, Mr. G.?" Jerry asked. "That fuckin' Hargrove. Do we tell 'im what we know?"

"We don't have to do his job for him," I said. "Let him figure it out."

I left him in the lobby and got back in the elevator.

***

"Eddie!" Danny Thomas said, when he opened his door. "Come on in."

"I hope I'm not interruptin' anythin'," I said.

"Not at all," Danny said. "I was on the phone discussing Make Room for Granddaddy, but I'm done for today. What's up?"

He was dressed casually, looking like he was ready for eighteen holes with grey slacks, a yellow polo shirt and white shoes.

"Hey, you want some coffee? I got a pot goin' behind the bar."

"No, thanks."

"Have a seat, then," Danny said. "You got some news for me?"

"I'm afraid I do."

Briefly, I told him what Jerry and I thought had happened. He listened intently, never interrupting, and didn't speak until I was done.

"I find this so hard to believe," he said. "Even though I gave you her name, I never really thought Susan could've done this. But you're right, why else would she have been killed?"

"The only other possibility I can see," I said, "is that somebody thought she stole the money and came after her for it."

"But why would she come to Vegas?" Danny asked. "No, I think you've convinced me that she took the money."

"Then what we have to do is find it and give it back to St. Jude."

"And what about finding her killer?" Danny asked. "Her partner?"

"That's up to the police," I said. "We just have to find the money."

Danny looked sad.

"I hope they find the killer," he said. "I always thought she was a nice kid. I still can't believe she's the one."

"Are you gonna stay in town?" I asked.

"I don't know how long it'll take you to find the money," he said, "but I'm confident you will, so I'll be around."

"I'll talk to Entratter about extending your stay in the suite," I said.

"Do you know who's coming in to play the room after me?" he asked.

"I'm not sure, but I think I heard Jack say something about Alan King."

"Oh, Alan's great," Danny said. "I'll have to stop in and see his show."

"I'll arrange it," I said. "Your ticket will be at the door."

He walked me to the door.

"Thanks, Eddie," Danny said, "for everything."

***

When I got back to the lobby, Penny was there talking to Jerry. She was smiling at him and touching his arm. When he saw me, he looked relieved.

"Hey, Mr. G.," he said. "She just got here."

"Hey, Eddie," Penny said.

"Where's the boss?" I asked.

"Are you kiddin'?" she asked. "You didn't really think I'd bring him here."

I looked at Jerry, who shrugged.

"Okay, Penny," I said, "I need you to go up, see the girls, get their sizes and buy them some clothes."

"For how long?"

"Just to be on the safe side," I said, "make it a week's worth each. Go to Francine's."

155

"That's one of the most expensive shops in town," she pointed out. "And what do I use for money?"

"Just charge it to the Sands."

"Okay, what room?"

I gave her the room number and she headed for the elevator.

"Penny."

She turned.

"While you're at Francine's, get something for yourself," I said.

She smiled. "I was going to."

Chapter Forty

I thought my next step should be to see Jack Entratter. For some reason, Jack wasn't crazy about Jerry, so I suggested he wait at the bar for me. He didn't argue. Guess the feeling must have been mutual.

When I got to Jack's office his girl said, "He's not there," before I could go in.

"Where is he?"

"At a meeting."

"Did he say where?" I asked. "With who?"

"No," she said, "he just told me to take messages."

"Did he say when he'd be back?"

"No."

I thought a moment, then simply left a message that Danny Thomas was going to need his suite a while longer and wanted a ticket to Alan King's show. She wrote it down.

"I'll make sure he gets it," she promised.

"Thank you."

***

I joined Jerry in the Silver Lounge, where he was sitting at the bar with a beer. I signaled the bartender to let me have one, as well.

"Entratter wasn't in his office," I said. "His girl says he's at a meeting somewhere. I left a message about Danny Thomas needing the suite longer."

"So whatta we do now?" he asked.

"That's a good goddamn question." I waved at the bartender. "Have another beer while we figure it out."

But before we could, Jack Entratter came in and headed straight for us. He didn't look happy.

"We need to talk," he said, when he reached us. "Alone."

"I'll finish my beer," Jerry said.

"Your office?" I asked Entratter.

"No," he said, "that table. Hey!" he snapped at the bartender. "Bring me a bourbon."

We walked to the table and sat. The bartender came over and put Entratter's bourbon down next to my half empty beer mug.

"Eddie?" he said.

"No, I'm good. Thanks."

He went back to the bar.

"What's up?" I asked.

"Hughes, goddamnit!" he growled.

"Is that who you had a meeting with?"

"No," he said, "I met with some of the other general managers. They say their bosses are entertaining offers from Hughes."

He drank half his bourbon.

"Okay, look," I said, "you're probably pissed at me, but I talked to them before you did. Frank and Dino also did some talking. Apparently, there's just too much money involved."

"Fuckin' Hughes," Entratter said. He sat back and took a deep breath. "What's goin' on with the Danny Thomas thing?"

"You didn't pick up your messages?"

"No," he said, "I came lookin' for you as soon as I got back."

I laid it out for him: what happened to the girls, putting them in a suite, what we thought it meant about Susan Morrow.

"Jesus Christ!" he said. "So she did steal the money?"

"Looks like it. And she must've had a partner or two."

"So if your buddy Jerry killed 'em, how do you plan on findin' the money?"

"I don't know," I said, "but I told Danny I'd find it and return it to St. Jude."

"Did you promise him that?" Entratter asked me. "Because if you did . . ."

"I didn't use the word 'promise,' " I said.

"And what about the murder?" Entratter asked. "If Hargrove finds you stickin' your nose in, he's gonna do his best to chop it off."

"I'm not lookin' into the murder, per se," I argued. "I'm lookin' for the money."

"I don't know if he's gonna see the difference," Entratter said. "Be careful, Eddie. I know I got you into this, but if you wanna walk away, I'll smooth it over with Danny."

"I'll stay on it, for now," I said.

He looked over at the bar.

"Is that big jamoke gonna stick with you?"

"All the way," I said. "He's in even deeper than I am, since he shot those two."

"Maybe you should send him back to Brooklyn?" Entratter suggested.

"Jack," I said, "there's no guarantee there isn't still somebody lookin' for that money. No, I'll keep Jerry here for a while."

"Yeah, okay." He finished his bourbon. "I'm goin' to my office. I've gotta make some calls."

"I'm gonna have another talk with Maheu," I said.

"And whataya think that will accomplish?" he asked, standing.

"Maybe nothin'," I said, "but it can't hurt."

***

"What'd he want?" Jerry asked when I got back to the bar.

"Well," I said, "among other things, he suggested I send you back to Brooklyn."

"We don't know how many other men are lookin' for that money. Mr. G.," Jerry said. "I ain't leavin' you alone."

"That's what I told him," I said. "He's also pissed because it looks like Hughes is gettin' some takers in his quest to buy up some properties."

"Things sure are changin' in this town, Mr. G.," Jerry observed.

"You said it, Jerry." I waved at the bartender again, this time motioning for a phone. He brought it over.

"Who you callin'?" Jerry asked.

"The D.I.," I said. "I told Jack I'd talk to Bob Maheu, again."

"On the phone?"

"Naw," I said, "with a guy like Maheu, you've gotta look him in the eye when you talk. I'm just settin' up."

"That's what I was gonna say."

Chapter Forty-One

Maheu not only came to the phone, but he agreed to meet me as long as it was somewhere else. I chose the Sahara. We didn't go into a restaurant or bar, but simply sat in the lobby, with plenty of people going this way and that.

"There's not much I can tell you, Eddie," he admitted. "Hughes is throwing money around like it's . . . confetti."

"I still don't think he's gonna be able to get any of the major properties."

"He's already got the Sands," Maheu said, "but you're right. "He's very close to making deals for the Castaway, the New Frontier and maybe the Landmark."

That was a relief. No Riv, no Sahara, no Flamingo. But who knew what would happen if he continued to raise his offers.

"And get this," Maheu said. "He's already bought The Silver Slipper just so he can move their neon sign."

"Why?"

"Apparently," Maheu went on, "he can see it from his bedroom window, and it keeps him awake at night."

"Jesus." I couldn't grasp what it must have been like to have *that* much money.

"Has he left the building?" I asked.

"No."

"Meetings?"

"Some here," Maheu said, "some I've gone out and taken."

"He trusts you that much?"

"Used to," Maheu said.

"What's that mean?"

"Just between you and me," he said, "I figure I'm on the way out."

"Why's that?"

"We're not seeing eye-to-eye lately."

"Do you object to the way he spends his money?" I asked.

"I've got no right to do that," Maheu said. "It's just like I said. We don't see eye-to-eye."

He obviously didn't want to say more than that on the subject, and I didn't think it was important for my purpose to pursue.

"You should know," Maheu said, "that he always gets what he wants. I know you and your pals have been trying to head him off, but it's not going to work." I knew by "pals" he meant Frank and Dino.

"I don't think that's gonna stop us from tryin'." I stood up. "Thanks for meeting me."

He also stood. Nobody paid us any attention.

"Those men who attacked you in the parking lot?"

"Yeah?"

"I didn't send them," Maheu said. "Neither did Hughes."

"Are you sure?"

"Yes."

"How?"

Maheu smiled.

"He likes you."

"You're kiddin'."

"I'm not. He'd give you a job if you asked."

"I won't."

"If you did," Maheu said, "you'd be well advised to save your pay. Nobody works for Hughes for very long."

"I'll keep that in mind."

We shook hands and I left. Jerry was outside with my Caddy. We had decided it would be better for him to wait there.

"Anythin'?" he asked as I got in.

"Not much luck," I said. "Looks like Hughes is definitely movin' in on Vegas."

"Aw hell," he said. "I like Vegas the way it is."

"I know," I said, "but life changes, and we have to change with it."

"Says who?" he grumbled.

Chapter Forty-Two

We had already concluded that Hughes had not sent the men to attack me in the parking lot, but it was nice to hear it from Maheu, anyway. No, those were the men who were looking for Susan Morrow and the St. Jude money. What we didn't know was if they were the same men who Jerry shot. In the parking lot there had been three, and Jerry had shot two. That left at least one more out there. We were still going to have to watch our own backs, as well as look after those girls: Lisa, Jennifer and Carol.

I decided it might be fruitful to talk to the girls again, in a calmer atmosphere than before, Carol specifically, got worked up. Maybe they're calmer after dealing with Penny.

I didn't know if Penny was still there or not, but Jerry and I took the elevator up, anyway. We knocked on the door of the suite, and it was answered by Jennifer, who was apparently in the midst of a laughing jag.

"Oh, hey," she said, trying to catch her breath, "come on in."

When we got inside, we saw what all the mirth was about. Penny was, indeed, still there, and all four girls had her purchases strewn about, as they were trying things on. Penny had apparently made good use of the Sands' credit line.

"Hey, Eddie," Penny said, "Jerry, we were just, uh, tryin' on some clothes."

"I can see that," I said.

Even Carol, the panicky one, was enjoying the fashion show.

"You wanna see some stuff?" she asked us, holding a glittery top up in front of her.

"We're gonna leave that to you girls," I said, "but we do have some questions."

"Is this about Susan?" Lisa asked.

"We hate to put a damper on your fun, but I'm afraid so."

Carol folded the top and set it down on the coffee table in front of the sofa.

"We shouldn't be havin' fun," she said. "Not with Susan dead and her killers still out there."

"Whataya wanna know, Eddie?" Lisa asked.

Penny stepped away to take a backseat.

"Whose friend was Susan?" I asked.

"Mine," Lisa said. "I introduced her to Jennifer and Carol."

"And did she call ahead to say she was coming, or just show up on your doorstep?"

I knew the answer, but I wanted to start with something simple.

"She just showed up at the door with a suitcase," Lisa said.

"One suitcase?"

"That was it."

"Don't take offense, ladies," I said, "but don't women usually travel with more than a single suitcase?"

"She said she packed in a hurry to get away from her scary boss. She said he kept hittin' on her and she had to get away."

"Did you think she was afraid?"

"She seemed to be," Jennifer said.

"Did you have any reason to think she was afraid for a more serious reason?"

"You mean," Lisa asked, "like maybe somebody wanted to kill her?"

"Not exactly," I said. "I don't think they were out to kill 'er. I think they wanted that St. Jude money, and it got out of hand."

"So you really think she stole all that money?" Lisa asked.

"That's how it looks," I said. "I think this is more than an amorous boss."

"How much is she supposed to have stolen?" Jennifer asked.

"I don't even know if there's a number," I said, "but it's a lot."

"Enough to kill for," Jerry said, speaking for the first time.

All three girls looked at him.

"What if Jerry stayed here with us," Lisa asked, "for a while, anyway."

"You're safe here," I told her.

"Mr. G.'s not safe out there," Jerry said. "I better stay with him."

"The killers might be after you?" Carol asked. "Why?"

"To keep me from findin' them," I said, "or the money."

"What about the police?" Carol asked.

"They're workin' on the murder."

"What about the money?" Jennifer asked.

"They might not know anything about it yet," I said.

"You haven't told them?" Lisa asked.

"No," I said, "the detective in charge and I, we don't get along."

"So he's working on the murder, and you're working on finding the money," Carol said. "Aren't you gonna meet in the middle at some point?"

"Maybe," I said. "I'll cross that bridge when we come to it."

"Won't he be pissed?" Carol asked.

"Oh yeah," I said, "but then, he always is."

"Are you sure we're safe here?" Jennifer asked.

"Nobody knows you're here," I said. "If they figure out that you are, at least they won't know what room. But just to be on the safe side, I'll talk to our hotel dick to keep an eye out."

The three girls exchanged a glance.

"Danny could do it," Penny said.

We all looked at her.

"My boss, Danny Bardini," Penny told them. "He's a private eye, and a good one."

Lisa looked at me.

"Would that be all right?" she asked.

"Danny's a friend of mine," I said. "I'll ask 'im."

"We'll ask him," Penny added. "He won't say no to both of us. I'll bring him around to meet all of you."

"Would he stay here with us?" Carol asked.

"Nearby," I said, before Penny could respond. "He'll keep an eye on you."

"Is there anything else?" Penny asked. "Or can we go back to our new clothes?"

"No," I said. "I think I have one more question." I looked at the girls. "Did Susan mention the St. Jude money to any of you?"

They all shook their heads,

"Not a word," Lisa said. "I wish she had. I would've told her to give it back."

"How long have you known her?" I asked.

"A long time," Lisa said. "I was born in Nashville. I moved here several years ago. I still can't believe she stole money from St. Jude."

"You can't believe she stole it?" I asked. "Or from St. Jude?"

"Both," Lisa answered. "It's just not like her."

"Okay." I looked at Penny. "I'll talk to Danny." I looked back at the girls. "We'll check on you again."

Penny walked us to the door.

"I'll tell Danny we said he'll keep an eye on them, not move in with 'em," I promised.

"Oh, don't worry," she said. "I'm going to tell him that myself."

As we went down in the elevator Jerry asked, "Can we trust the shamus with those girls?"

"Oh, don't worry," I said. "He knows Penny would cut off his dick if he tried anything."

"She's such a nice girl."

"That may be," I said, "but you can only push nice girls so far."

Chapter Forty-Three

When the elevator doors opened, and Jerry started to step out, I immediately spotted Detective Hargrove across the lobby. I could tell
from his walk he was pissed, but it was like I had told the girls, he was
always pissed.

I grabbed Jerry's arm and yanked him back into the elevator.

"What the fuck, Mr. G.?" he asked, as the doors closed.

"Hargrove's in the lobby," I said. "I don't want to deal with him,
right now."

"So whataya wanna do?"

"We'll get off on two and take the stairs," I said. "Then we'll see if
we can duck out the back without him seeing."

"You think he's lookin' for you, or me?"

"One's just as bad as the other."

The elevator doors opened at two and I led the way to the stairs. We
went down, and I peered out the door before waving Jerry to follow me.
Instead of going into the lobby, we went out the back door to the rear
parking lot. Since I'd already been jumped in the back lot, we had
parked on the side of the building.

"Where to?" Jerry asked as we got in the car.

"I was gonna call Danny," I said, "but now we might as well go to
his office."

"Right," Jerry said. "Fremont Street."

We parked behind the Horseshoe.

"Any chance of eatin' here?" Jerry asked. He really liked the Horseshoe's coffee shop.

"Sure," I said. "We'll invite Danny."

The downstairs door was unlocked, so we took the stairs to Danny's office. That door was locked, so we knocked.

"Where's my girl?" Danny asked, when he opened the door.

"Come on," Jerry said. "We'll buy you some food and tell ya."

"Deal," Danny said. He stepped out, pulled the door shut, locked it, and we walked to the Horseshoe. If you liked the coffee shop the way Jerry did, the ride down on the escalator was filled with anticipation.

We got a booth and all ordered burger platters. Danny and I sat on one side, while Jerry's bulk filled the other seat.

"When can I have Penny back?" Danny asked.

"Actually," I said, "that's why we're here. We need somebody to keep an eye on the three girls."

"Showgirls?"

"I think two are showgirls and one's a waitress, but yeah," I said.

"And you want me to babysit 'em?"

"It was really Penny's idea."

"You're kiddin'!"

"No," I said, "the girls are scared, so I told 'em I'd have the house dick keep an eye on 'em, but Penny said you'd do it."

"What a sweet kid."

"But she said you'd do it from outside the suite, not inside."

Danny laughed.

"Now that makes more sense. Is this a payin' job, or another favor?"

"Well," I said, "since Penny offered . . ."

"A favor, then," Danny said. "Okay, do I at least get to meet the girls?"

"Sure," I said, "but we'll let Penny introduce you."

"So she can keep an eye on you," Jerry said, with a grin.

"Penny's in the suite with 'em now; so you can head over there after we eat."

We all leaned back to allow the waitress to set the plates down.

"Is this still the Danny Thomas thing?" Danny asked.

"Yeah, it is."

We filled him in on what we thought was going on, while he ate and listened.

"It makes sense to me," he said, when I finished. "It'd be too much of a coincidence that she gets killed and it's not about the money."

Danny was a good detective, and I was happy to have his approval about our theory.

"So you're lookin' for the money," he said.

"Right."

"Does Hargrove know what you're doin'?"

"I don't know," I said. "He was at the Sands a little while ago, and we avoided him."

"You know you're gonna have to deal with him sooner or later," Danny pointed out.

"I'm hopin' to make it later," I admitted.

"Maybe he was lookin' for Jerry," Danny said. "He might wanna return his gun."

Hargrove had hung on to Jerry's .45. He'd give it back eventually, but I doubted that was why the cop had been at the Sands.

I filled Danny in on who the girls were, which one was the dead girl's friend while the others were her roommates. Jerry ate all his fries, but I didn't bug him about it. He was a big boy and had been dealing with his diabetes for some time.

"How many mugs am I watchin' for?" Danny asked.

"Three jumped me in the parking lot, and Jerry shot two. That might mean only one's left, but my feeling is those three were knuckle dusters workin' for somebody else."

"So we don't know."

"Can't be sure."

"Okay," Danny said, "good to know."

We went back outside and went our separate ways in front of the Horseshoe.

"If I see Hargrove when I get there," Danny said, "I haven't seen ether one of you."

"That'll work," I said.

Danny went his way, and we went back to my car.

Chapter Forty-Four

"What's up, Mr. G.?" Jerry asked. "You ain't said a word since we got in the car."

"I'm havin' a thought."

"About what?"

"The three girls," I said.

"All three?" he asked. "Pick one, for Chrissake."

"No," I said, "I'm wonderin' if Susan Morrow came here and really didn't say anythin' about the money to her friends."

"You think the girls were in on it?" Jerry asked.

"I don't know if they were in on it," I said, "but maybe they know more than they're sayin'. For instance, Carol was real panicky when we first met her, and now she seems to be in perfect control of herself."

"She was the one with the most questions," Jerry said. "But Lisa was Susan's friend."

"I know," I said. "If they were so close that Susan came to her, is she really totally ignorant of what was goin' on?"

"Do you wanna ask her?"

"I think maybe we should go and have another look in their apartment."

"Right now?"

I nodded.

"Yeah, right now."

"You got it."

He hit the brakes, executed a quick U-turn that made my heart leap into my throat.

***

We told the doorman, Vincent, the girls had sent us to pick up some items, and he let us into their apartment.

"I gotta get back down to my desk," he told us.

"We won't be long," I promised.

He nodded and left us alone.

"What are we lookin' for, Mr. G.?" Jerry asked.

"Anything that confirms what we were just talkin' about," I said. "I'll check the bedrooms. You do here and the kitchen."

"Right."

There were three bedrooms. In my mind I assigned one to each girl. One room was neat and tidy. I figured that for Lisa. A search turned up a few family photos and letters, which told me I was right. There were no letters from Susan Morrow.

The second room was a mess, articles of clothing strewn about as if they'd been thrown off in a hurry. I figured that one for Jennifer, who always looked a bit messy. Once again, I found some photos telling me I was right, but that was all I found.

So the third bedroom belonged to Carol. Not as neat as Lisa's, but not the mess Jennifer's was. I found photos and letters, and some notes on a pad that indicated Carol had some appointments to try out for some casino shows. One was at the Flamingo and another at the Riviera. I recognized the names of the directors of the shows, women I had come to know over the years.

I found Jerry sitting in the living room, eating a sandwich.

"Where'd you get that?"

"In the kitchen," he said, with his mouth full. "I found some ham in the frig that's on the verge of goin' bad. Some bread, too, so I rescued 'em." He held the sandwich up as if in a salute, then took another big bite. "What'd you find, Mr. G.?"

"Not much," I admitted, "certainly nothing helpful as far as Susan Morrow's concerned. But I did think of a few more questions we can ask."

"Who we gonna question?"

"I'll tell you on the way," I said. "Did you find any bags?"

"What kind?"

"Just a shopping bag would do," I told him. "We can toss some stuff into it so Vincent sees that we left with somethin'."

"I saw some in the kitchen."

He went to the kitchen, came back with a good-sized shopping bag.

"Whataya wanna put in it?" he asked.

I opened it, looked around, took one of the throw pillows off the sofa and stuffed it inside.

"That'll do," I said.

He finished his sandwich on the way down in the elevator. I held the shopping bag up as we passed Vincent's desk and said, "Thanks."

On the street Jerry asked, "Where we goin' now?"

"First to the Riv," I said, "then the Flamingo."

"What's there?"

As we got back in the car I said, "I found some notes showing that Carol has been trying out for some shows. I just want to talk to the directors about her."

"She's the waitress, right?"

"Yeah."

"A little chubby to be a showgirl, ain't she?"

"That's what I want to find out."

Chapter Forty-Five

We hit the Riviera first. The directors for the shows changed frequently. Nora Wilson had gotten a job a year ago. A longtime dancer herself, the shows didn't often feature women in their forties. So Nora worked her way up the ladder until she was in charge.

We parked and went inside. I found out that Nora was presently rehearsing the girls in the showroom. As Jerry and I entered from the back, we could see the line of girls on stage, going through their steps, with Nora watching from the front row. We went down the aisle and I slid in next to her while Jerry took a seat behind her.

She took a quick look to see who it was and smiled at me.

"Hey, Eddie," she said, "come to watch me put my girls through their paces?"

"They look good."

"Some do," she said. "Watch that one on the end, to the right?"

It was a pretty brunette with long legs clad in fishnet stockings.

"What about her?"

"She's constantly a half step behind," Nora said. "I'm gonna have to let her go."

"Does that mean you'll need a replacement?"

"Oh yeah," she said, "luckily there's no shortage of girls lookin' for jobs." She studied the stage again. "Okay, everybody, take five!"

She took a deep breath and looked at me. Her dark hair was piled up on top of her head, and her pretty blue eyes stared at me from behind her tortoise shell glasses.

"What brings you here?"

"A girl named Carol Peters," I said. I'd gotten her last name off a letter in her room.

"Who is she? A girlfriend who needs a job?"

"No, nothin' like that," I said. "But I do know that she had an appointment with you. I assume it was to audition."

"Carol . . . what's she look like?"

"Blonde, twenties, kinda pretty. . ."

". . . and a little chubby," Jerry put in.

Nora raised her eyebrows.

"Now I remember," she said. "Your friend's right, I told her she was too . . . chubby for our line."

"How did she take that?"

"Not well," Nora admitted. "She got angry, said it wasn't fair, that she was only about ten pounds overweight."

"And you said?"

"I said she needed to lose more like twenty, and then come back. She stormed off."

"And that was it?" I asked. "You never heard from her again?"

"Not a word," Nora said. "That was about . . . oh, two weeks ago."

"Okay," I said, "thanks."

"I guess you think that was cruel," she said.

"Not cruel," I said, "just direct." I stood up. "Thanks, Nora."

"You're welcome."

She was clapping her hands and calling the girls back on stage as we left.

***

The Flamingo was next.

Daisy Kellogg had been the director there for years. She was in her late forties now, and, as we entered her office, she took off her glasses and let them dangle on her chest by a chain.

"Eddie G.," she said. "And friend?"

"Daisy, this is Jerry," I said.

"Hello, Jerry."

She came around from behind her desk to give me a hug.

"Have a seat, boys," she said, returning to her seat. "What's on your mind?"

"A girl named Carol Peters," I said. "I believe she auditioned for your line."

"Blonde, pudgy?" Daisy asked.

"That's her," Jerry said.

"That was two or three weeks ago," Daisy said. "I had to tell her she wasn't Flamingo material."

"How'd she take it?"

"She stormed out of here and slammed the door."

"Did she say anything?"

"Just one thing."

"What was it?"

"She said, 'I've had enough.' "

"What did you think that meant?"

Daisy shrugged.

"Enough rejection, I guess," she said. "I can't think of a line that would take 'er. These girls have to be thick-skinned to take rejection. I got the feeling she was only thick-hipped."

Chapter Forty-Six

"So what'd we find out?" Jerry asked, as we drove back to the Sands.

"Carol's a frustrated showgirl," I said. "And she's tired of being rejected."

"You think she knows where the money is?"

"I think if she did, she'd see it as a way out," I said. "She wouldn't need to work anymore, not as a waitress and not as a showgirl."

"What about the other two?"

"You'd think if one of the girls knew about the money it'd be Lisa," I said.

"So if one, two or all the girls knew about it, do you think they woulda killed 'er for it?"

"That wasn't what I was thinkin'," I said. "I figure somebody else killed Susan, but the girls might know where she was keepin' the money."

"I'd like that better," Jerry said. "Lisa and Jennifer seem too nice."

"But Carol . . ."

"Yeah," Jerry said, "I don't like Carol, either."

"I guess we better go and talk to them."

***

Danny Bardini was in the lobby, talking to one of the bellmen.

"Did you meet the girls?" I asked.

"Yeah, Penny introduced us. She's still up there, by the way. What's up?"

"Some more questions," I said. "We're wonderin' if one or more of them knows where the money is."

"Want me to come up with you?"

"No, that's okay," I said. "Have you seen Hargrove today?"

"No."

"Well, do me a favor, if you do see him, give us a heads up."

"You got it."

Jerry and I took the elevator up and knocked on the suite door. It was opened by Penny, who was holding her purse.

"I was just leaving," she said. "Do you want me to stay?"

"No, that's okay," I said. "You've done enough. Thanks, Penny."

"You're welcome."

She stepped out and headed for the elevator, and we stepped in.

"Hey, boys!" Jennifer said, holding her arms out. "Whataya think?" She had a colorful skirt and matching top on.

"Very nice," I said.

"Your friend Penny has good taste," she said. "Come in, the girls are at the bar."

Lisa was behind the bar, Carol sitting in front, both wearing new clothes. They each held a highball glass.

"What's goin' on, Eddie?" Lisa asked. "Can we go home, yet?"

"I hope not," Carol said, with a grin. "I like it here. Is this the kind of suite Frank Sinatra stays in?"

"Pretty much."

"You guys want a drink?" Lisa asked. "We got a fully stocked bar. Jerry?"

"Bottle of beer, if ya got it."

"In the frig." Lisa opened the small refrigerator and took out a bottle of Piels. "Eddie?"

"Bourbon, neat."

"Comin' up."

She put Jerry's beer on the bar, poured my bourbon. We both walked over and picked up our drinks.

"We met Penny's boss, Danny," Jennifer said. "He's very handsome. Why doesn't he stay in here with us?"

"Come on, Lisa," Carol said, "you know why. He's her guy. You think she wants to share him with us?"

"I wouldn't mind," Jennifer said, coming over to the bar.

"Danny's keepin' an eye on you girls," I said. "We're here to ask a few more questions."

"What questions?" Lisa asked.

"About Susan and the money."

"Oh, that," Lisa said. "I'm still not convinced she really stole that money."

"Well, actually," I said, "I want to talk to each of you individually. We can use one of the bedrooms."

Lisa and Jennifer looked confused. Carol, however, seemed concerned.

"Why separately?" she asked. "Do you think we'd have different stories?"

"I just don't want one of your answers to influence the others."

"Girls," Carol said, "I don't think this is a good idea. I think we should stay together."

"I think I'd like to start with Carol," I said. "Jerry will keep you other two girls company."

"What if I don't want to go in the other room with you?" Carol asked.

"Then I'll have Jerry take the girls into the other room and you and I will talk here," I said.

"It's not a problem, Carol," Lisa said.

"Yeah, go ahead," Jennifer said. "We'll stay here with Jerry."

"Carol," I said, and waved for her to precede me.

Chapter Forty-Seven

"What's this really about?" Carol demanded as I closed the bedroom door. "And can you leave that door open, please?"

I opened it, but not all the way. If either of us had wanted to sit, it would have to be on the bed, so we remained standing.

"Carol," I said, "we know that you've been auditioning for shows on the strip, and they keep rejecting you."

"Oh yeah?" she asked. "So the word's gotten around, huh? Did they tell you why they rejected me?"

"Somethin' about your weight, isn't it?" I asked.

"And do you think I look fat?" She held her arms out.

"Well," I said, "not fat, but those showgirls are kinda long and lean."

"There's nothin' I can do about my damn height," she said. "It's not fair."

"Guess you'll just have to keep tryin'."

"I'm tired of tryin'," she said. "And what do you care, anyway?"

"I was just lookin' into the background of you girls," I said.

"Why?" Carol frowned. "Do you think we had somethin' to do with Susan's murder?"

"No," I said, "maybe not the murder . . ."

"Oh," she said, "the money, then."

"Well," I said, "if Susan did tell you where the money was, would you turn it in?"

"Oh, I get it," she said. "Because I'm a failed dancer, you think I'd steal the money."

"I didn't say that—"

"But that's what you mean," she said, cutting me off. "Are you gonna ask Jen and Lisa the same questions?"

"I am," I said. "Are they gonna get as upset as you?"

"Look," she said, "I didn't really know Susan, all right? She was Lisa's friend. In fact, I didn't even like her."

"Why not?"

"She was a stuck-up bitch!" Carol hissed. "Lookin' down her nose at me—us."

"So, if you knew where the money was—"

"I don't!" she snapped. "I'm done, here!"

She headed for the door.

"Do me a favor and ask Jennifer to come back here."

She stormed out, and I heard her shout something unintelligible. Then I heard her say, "He wants you!"

Jennifer came into the room, looking puzzled.

"What did you say to Carol to get her so worked up?" she asked.

"We talked about her auditions."

"Oh!" Jennifer said, her eyes wide. "We try not to talk to her about those. She's sensitive about her weight."

"I get that," I said, "but tell me, Jennifer, what do you think Carol would do if she found that money?"

"We talked about that," she said. "We even looked all over our apartment, thinking maybe Susan hid it there. We all agreed we'd give it back." She sat on the bed and shrugged. "It seems like that would be the right thing to do."

"Okay," I said, "that's if all three of you found it. What do you think Lisa or Carol would do if they found the money, and didn't tell you?"

"Is that what you think?"

"I'm graspin' at straws here, Jennifer," I said. "Just humor me."

"Well . . . Lisa would give it back."

"And Carol?"

Jennifer looked at the bedroom door, then got up and closed it before sitting back down again.

"Eddie," she said, "Carol's been in a real bad mood lately. She hates bein' a waitress, and nobody'll take her on as a showgirl."

"So, if she found the money," I asked, "just . . . stumbled on it, what would she do?"

"She'd probably . . . well, she might . . . keep it," Jennifer said, with a shrug.

"But not Lisa?"

"Oh, Lisa is so honest."

"And if I ask Lisa the same question, what would she say about you?"

Jennifer thought about it for a moment, then said, "I'd hope she'd say I'd give it back."

***

"She'd give it back," Lisa said, immediately.

Like Jennifer, Lisa didn't hesitate to close the bedroom door. "But Carol, she'd keep it."

"You're sure?"

"I'm positive."

"How can you be?"

"She told me."

"When?"

"One night, after Susan disappeared, Jen was out. Carol and I were home, alone. We talked about it. Carol said it sounded like there was enough money so that we wouldn't have to work. We could keep it and split it. So how much are we talkin' about Eddie? You never said."

I never said because I didn't know at the time.

"Susan never told you?"

"She only said she stole some money and didn't know what to do with it. She was leaning toward givin' it back."

"She told all three of you about the money?"

Lisa bit her lip.

"No," she said, "only me. She didn't know the other girls well enough to trust them."

"But you did, or, you thought you did."

"It never occurred to me Carol would want to keep the money."

"How did she plan on taking it from Susan?"

"I don't know," she said. "We never discussed that. She wanted to find out how much it was, first."

"And Susan wouldn't tell you?"

"She hadn't told me yet, then she disappeared."

"So you and the other girls don't know how much she took, or where it is?"

"No," Lisa said, "we don't."

"All right," I said. "Let's go back to the others."

"Will you still keep us safe here?" she asked.

"For as long as I can."

We left the bedroom and joined the others. The two girls were sitting on the sofa, and Jerry was seated at the bar.

"All right," I said. "All three of you, stay put. We'll be back tomorrow."

We left the suite. It was getting late, so I told Jerry to turn in and I'd spend the night in the hotel and meet up with him in the morning.

Chapter Forty-Eight

The next morning, I decided to call Danny Thomas from my hotel room before meeting Jerry for breakfast.

"What do you need, Eddie?" Danny asked.

"I'm wonderin' how much money we're talkin' about, Danny," I said. "Do you have an exact amount?"

"Not really," he said. "I mean, I could get it—"

"Can you do that and let me know?" I asked.

"I'll make some calls," Danny said. "Do you have an idea of where it is?"

"I've got several ideas, but I think a lot is gonna depend on how much is involved."

"Give me a call later today," he said. "I'll have an answer for you."

"Okay, thanks."

I hung up, went down and met Jerry in the Garden Room.

"Let's eat," I said.

"No argument from me, Mr. G."

We sat and ordered. Then I told him about calling Danny Thomas.

"You thinkin' if it was enough these girls might be hidin' it?" he asked, once we were settled at the bar.

"I'm thinkin' if Susan and Lisa were truly good friends, Susan might've confided in her."

"And then Lisa told the others?"

"Maybe."

"So how do we figure it out?" Jerry asked. "We can't follow 'em because they're here in the hotel."

"It wouldn't do any good to check bank accounts," I said. "They wouldn't have put stolen money into the bank under their own names."

"What if they split it up?" Jerry asked.

"It would still be too much," I said, "but we'll know more when I hear from Danny how much we're really talkin' about."

"Then we can't do anythin' until then," Jerry said.

"Probably not."

"So what do we do in the meantime?" Jerry asked.

I looked past him and said, "This might be an answer to that question."

Jerry turned to see what I was looking at. It was actually "who," as Robert Maheu was walking toward us.

"We need to talk," he said seriously, when he reached us. "Alone."

"Anything you need to say to me you can say in front of Jerry," I said. "Besides, we're having breakfast, as you can see."

"Then let's move to a table."

"Coffee?" I asked him.

He nodded and sat next to me in the booth as I poured it for him.

"What's on your mind?"

"Somebody tried to kill Hughes," he said.

"What?"

"Took a shot at him last night," Maheu said.

"I thought Hughes wasn't leaving the D.I."

"He didn't," Maheu said. "Somebody got in."

"Then how did they miss?"

"A bellboy happened to be bringing up an order at the time," Maheu said. "He interrupted the shooter, threw off his shot."

"What happened?"

"He cold-cocked the bellboy and ran off. Hughes called me immediately, but the shooter got away."

"Who do you think it was?"

"I think it was a pro," Maheu said.

"A hitter?" Jerry said. "Who put out a hit on Howard Hughes?"

Maheu looked at me.

"That's what I want you to find out," he said. "And I want the hit taken off."

"What makes you think I can do that?"

"Because you're Mister Vegas," he said. "And this has to be a mob hit."

"Why? Because Hughes is buyin' casinos? That's a little far-fetched, don't you think?"

"No," Maheu said, "I don't think. Vegas is owned by the mob, Eddie, and now Hughes is trying to move in."

"And you think they'd put out a high profile hit like that?" I said. "I don't see it."

"Okay then," Maheu said, "this is your town. Prove me wrong by finding out who *did* put the hit out."

He downed his coffee, rose and stalked off.

"Are you gonna do it?" Jerry asked, finishing his last bite of pan-cakes.

"As if we didn't have enough to do," I said.

"I could ask around," Jerry offered.

I looked at him. Maybe Vegas was my town, but the world of mob hits was more his bailiwick than mine.

"Okay," I said, "I'll talk to Entratter and see what he knows, but go ahead, make your calls."

"Right."

"Do it from your room," I said. "I'll come there after I've talked to Jack."

Chapter Forty-Nine

"A hit?" Jack Entratter repeated. "Who do you think is gonna put a hit out on Howard Hughes? I'm not sure what I think."

"Hughes and Maheu think it was a mob hit."

Entratter stared at me from behind his desk.

"If it was a mob hitter, Hughes would be dead," he reasoned. "They don't miss."

"Then who do you suppose put out the hit?"

"Could've been anybody," Entratter said. "One of the other casino people. Any of them could've decided this was the way to stop Hughes. In fact, it could even have been—" He stopped short.

"No," I said, "not Frank."

"Of course not," Entratter said. "I just meant . . . it could be any-body."

I stared at him. If he knew who the mob hitter was, would he tell me? I had often thought Jack and I were friends, but the fact was he worked for the mob, and I worked for him.

"Okay," I said, "I guess I'm just gonna have to keep lookin'."

I stood up.

"That might not be a good idea, Eddie," Entratter said.

"You wanna tell me why?"

"I'm . . . just sayin'."

I remembered as a kid growing up in Brooklyn many people explained themselves with the words, "I'm just sayin'."

"Yeah, okay," I said.

"Besides," Entratter added, "you still have Danny Thomas' problem to work on."

"Right," I said. "I have to call him and find out just how much money was taken."

"Are those girls still in one of our suites?"

"Yeah," I said. "Just for a while longer, until Hargrove catches the killer."

"You think he will?"

"I guess he'd better," I said. "It's his case."

"Okay," Entratter said, "just . . . get that suite freed up as soon as possible."

"I will."

I left his office and took the elevator to Jerry's floor. When he opened the door for me, he said, "You ain't gonna believe this."

I walked in and saw that a room service cart had been wheeled in. On it were two plates of burgers and fries. I felt like we'd only just had breakfast, but that never stopped Jerry.

"Is this all right?" Jerry asked.

"I might've ordered steak," I said, "but sure, it's fine. Let's eat and you can tell me what it is I won't believe."

We sat down and picked up our burgers. Or, rather, Jerry grabbed his burger and I picked at my fries.

"It only took a few well-placed calls," Jerry said. "I found out a guy named Willie the Wolf Frankel took the contract."

"Why do they call him the Wolf?" I asked.

"That's what he calls himself," Jerry said. "He's third rate, at best. None of the families would use him."

"So you're sayin' this wasn't a mob sanctioned bit?"

"No," Jerry said, "it wasn't. Somebody here in Vegas offered the contract and Willie grabbed it. I'm not surprised he missed."

"Would you know him on sight?"

"I would."

"So all we have to do is find Willie, and ask him who's payin' him."

"That's what I was thinkin'." Jerry admitted.

"Good work, Jerry."

"Thanks, Mister G."

We both bit into our burgers.

***

After we finished eating, I called Danny Thomas.

"Three hundred thousand, Eddie," he told me.

"Jesus."

"I know," Danny said. "I didn't realize it was that much. That'd tempt anybody, even someone like Susan."

"And whoever killed her."

"Yeah, right," Danny said, "whoever killed her. Have you got a line on that, yet?"

"I've got some ideas," I said, "especially now that I know how much is at stake. I'll be in touch."

We hung up and I turned to Jerry.

"Three hundred kay," I said.

"Holy shit!" he snapped. "If she stole that much, where the hell did she put it before she was killed?"

"That's the question."

"But . . . what if she didn't take it?"

"Keep talkin'," I said.

"What if somebody thought she took it, and ended up killin' her when she didn't have it?"

I thought a moment, then said, "What's she doin' in Vegas, then? Lisa said she wasn't a gambler."

"She also said she came here to party and see shows."

"And she said Susan was scared," I reminded him.

"Yeah, and she said Susan loved St. Jude and would never steal from the place."

"And what would change the mind of a young woman who likes to party?"

"I don't kn—oh, wait. You mean . . . a man?"

I nodded.

"A man who convinced her to steal the money, and then killed her for it."

"But . . . he ain't got it, or I wouldn't have had to kill those bums in Lisa's apartment."

"Right," I said, "the money's still out there, somewhere."

"So we're gonna keep lookin' for the money," Jerry said, "while we look for Willie the Wolf?"

"Exactly," I said.

"So where do we go from here? I wanna ask my buddy, Danny, again about the other two St. Jude trustees, who happen to be men."

Chapter Fifty

One call told us Danny Bardini was in his Fremont Street office. He said he'd meet us in the Horseshoe, but I apologized and said we didn't have time, we agreed to talk in his office.

When we entered half-an-hour later, Penny said, "He's waiting for you."

"Thanks, Penny," I said, "but what's he doin' here? He's supposed to be watchin' the girls at the Sands,"

"Yes, I heard about that," she said, sternly. "We've got a good man on the job. Don't worry."

I decided not to argue with her.

We entered the inner office.

"There you are," Danny said. "What's this about? Hughes?"

"St. Jude."

"Oh, that."

"I have a question," I said. "The girl, Susan . . . could she have been havin' a romantic relationship?"

"Only if she likes older men," Danny said. "Why?"

"Her friends seem to think she stole the money from St. Jude for love."

Jerry and I sat across from Danny.

"That may be," Danny said, "but I can't see it bein' Hector Dominguez or Clarence Foster."

"Then there may be a younger man involved, somehow."

"You want me to look into that?"

"If you have the time," I said.

"I can make time," Danny said. "I'd like to help Mr. Thomas any way I can."

"When this is over," I said, "I'll make sure you meet him so he can say thank you."

"I'll hold you to that."

I looked at Jerry.

"We better get goin'."

"Where are you off to?" Danny asked.

"Jerry thinks he knows who the hitman was who tried to kill Hughes," I said.

"Whoa, back up," Danny said. "That's news to me."

"Geez, I'm sorry," I said. "I forgot to tell you, Maheu came to me . . ." I explained what Maheu had said, and how we had agreed to help get the hit removed.

"But according to Entratter and Jerry, it's not a sanctioned hit?"

"That's right," I said. "We figure somebody in town initiated it."

Danny sat back in his chair.

"Would it be such a bad thing?" he asked.

"Come again?"

"If Hughes was killed, then he wouldn't be around to buy casinos. I mean, isn't that what we want?"

"We may not want him buyin' up Vegas," I pointed out, "but that doesn't mean we want him dead."

***

We left Danny's office after agreeing he would find out if Susan Morrow had a boyfriend.

"Now whatta we do?" Jerry asked as we hit the street

"We find Willie the Wolf," I said. "Only where do we start lookin'?"

"That's what I was gonna ask you," Jerry said. "This is your town."

"Okay," I said, "if we were in Brooklyn, where would you look?"

"Now you're talkin'," Jerry said. "Since he's not a top-level hitter, I'd check flophouses, YMCAs, rooming house—"

"Why not a better Hotel?"

"Whatever he's gettin' paid, he wouldn't waste it on a hotel. He just needs a room to hole up in, and sleep if he has to."

"Well, there are plenty of places for that off the strip," I pointed out.

"It'd take us a while to check them all out," Jerry said.

And we didn't have Danny Bardini to recruit for help.

"So whatta we do?"

"Recruit some new help," I said. "How well can you describe Willie the Wolf?"

Chapter Fifty-One

When we pulled into the Sands hotel parking lot, I noticed Buddy Greco's name on the marque, with Charlie Callas opening for him. That told me I was out of the loop, because I didn't know Buddy was coming in.

"He any good?" Jerry asked.

"Who?"

"That Greco guy."

"He's okay," I said. "He's no Vic Damone."

"Who?"

"Forget it."

We parked but didn't go inside. Instead, I led the way around to the front, where the valets were standing.

"These guys?" Jerry asked.

"One of 'em."

"Which one?"

I watched as the valets ran to a car and drove off, then came running back.

"Which one?" Jerry asked, again.

I pointed.

"That one."

"I don't know 'im," Jerry said.

"I got him the job last month," I said.

"What was he doin' before that?"

"B-and-Es," I said. "I convinced him that a real job would keep him outta jail."

"So he'll have some connections?"

"That's what I'm thinkin'," I said. "Let's talk to him. His name's Jimmy."

We walked over to where he was standing with two other valets.

"Jimmy?" I asked.

He turned and smiled when he saw me. He was young—under twenty-five—tall, thin, agile enough to pull burglaries on upper floors, until he got caught.

"Hey, Eddie G.!" he said, loudly. "What can I do for you, man?"

"I need a favor," I said. "Can we talk?"

"I'll be right back," he told the other valets, who both waved at me. I returned the wave.

Jerry and I walked Jimmy over to a spot where we wouldn't be overheard.

"You still got contacts, Jimmy?" I asked.

"Hey, Mr. G.," he said, "you got me this job and I ain't broke the law since, I swear."

"But you still know people, right?"

Jimmy frowned.

"Contacts?"

"People who are still breakin' the law?"

"Well," Jimmy said, "I do have some friends. What do you need?"

"We're lookin' for somebody who goes by the name Willie the Wolf."

Jimmy laughed, then said, "For real?"

I looked at Jerry.

"Willie's a low-level hitman, takes jobs the major hitters won't, doesn't work for anybody with smarts."

"So the families don't hire 'im?" Jimmy asked.

"Never," Jerry said.

"Then what's he doin' in Vegas?" Jimmy asked.

"He's been hired to kill Howard Hughes."

Jimmy stared at me and said, "Jesus Christ!"

"We're tryin' to stop him," I said. "The only way we can do that is to find him."

"And you want my help?" Jimmy asked. "What can I do?"

"Put the word out among your friends," I said. "We believe Willie will be holed up in a flophouse somewhere,"

"Or worse," Jerry added.

"Ah, I get it, now," Jimmy said. "You think my friends hang out in those places."

"Your old friends," I said, "not the ones you've made since workin' here."

"I'll need a detailed description," Jimmy said.

I left that to Jerry, and he painted a picture with his words that would make Willie hard to miss.

"I assume you want this soon?" Jimmy asked when Jerry was done.

"As soon as possible," I said.

"I'll have to take some time off," Jimmy said.

"I'll arrange it," I said.

"Where do I find you when I have somethin'?" he asked.

"Either, here, or leave me a message at the front desk," I said. "we'll be checkin' in."

"Tell me," Jimmy said, "what are you gonna do with him when you find him?"

"Stop him," I said.

"Uh-huh. Okay, Mr. G.," Jimmy said. "I'll get right on it."

He turned and took off at a run.

"What makes you think he's gonna have the friends to make this work, Mr. G.?" Jerry asked.

"It was Jimmy's friends who got him on the wrong track in the first place."

"What if this puts him back there?"

"I don't think that'll happen," I said, "but if it does, I'll have to take full responsibility."

Chapter Fifty-Two

I had Danny Bardini looking for a boyfriend of Susan Morrow's, and Jimmy and his friends looking for a third-rate hitman named Willie the Wolf. That left Jerry and me to find the money. If we could do that, whoever was working with Susan Morrow would come to us.

The only possible connection we had to the money appeared to be the three girls we still had in a Sands suite.

"Which one?" Jerry asked, as we sat in the lounge.

"Which one . . . what?" I asked.

"Which girl do you think knows where the money is?"

"Well, Lisa was Susan's friend," I answered. "She's the one Susan would have confided in."

"But you don't think it's her, do you?"

"If it is, then she's been lyin' to us," I said. "I don't see her as a liar."

"Neither do I," Jerry said. "She's a sweet kid."

"So is Jennifer."

"Then that leaves the blonde, Carol," Jerry said.

"She seems to have harder edges than the others," I observed.

"I agree," he said.

"But why would Susan have told her where the money was when it was Lisa she was friends with?" I asked.

"Maybe," Jerry said, "we should ask her."

I drained my scotch and set the glass down on the bar.

"Good idea."

***

"She's gone!" Lisa exclaimed, as soon as she opened the door for us.

"What?"

"Carol," Lisa said, backing up so we could enter. "She's gone. We couldn't stop her!"

Jennifer was seated on the sofa, hugging herself.

"She's gonna get herself killed, isn't she?" she asked.

"Not if we can help it," I said. "Do you have any idea where she'd go?"

"None," Lisa said, sitting next to Jennifer, so close that their shoulders were touching.'

"Why would she leave?" I asked.

Lisa and Jennifer exchanged a glance, and then Lisa said, "We don't know. She just said she had to get out."

This time Jerry and I exchanged a glance. We believed the two girls.

"What are the chances Carol knows where the money is," I asked, "and went to get it?"

"I don't see how, Eddie," Lisa said. "If Susan wouldn't tell me where it was, why would she tell Carol?"

"That's a good question," I said.

"But," Jennifer said, "how will you find her?"

"I don't know," I said. "We'll figure somethin' out. Meanwhile, promise me the two of you will stay here?"

"Oh, we'll stay," Lisa said. "We don't wanna get killed."

"Please, Eddie," Jennifer said, "find Carol and bring her back."

"We'll do our best," I said.

Out in the hall, on the way to the elevator, Jerry said, "How *are* we gonna find 'er?"

"Beats me," I said, "but we're gonna give it the ol' college try."

***

Tracking Carol turned out to be easy. We found Danny's man, a P.I. I knew named Stan Baker. He was immediately ashamed that the girl had gotten out of the hotel without him seeing her. I told him to stay on the job. He promised nothing would happen to the other two girls.

We hit the valets again, and one of them had put her into a cab.

"Who's cab?" I asked.

"Blue Flamingo Cab Company," the valet said. "The driver was Artie Muranto."

"You know 'im?" Jerry asked.

"I know 'im," I said.

"Know where he is?"

"Probably drivin' around," I said. "That means he'll be back here."

We told the valet we'd be inside. When Muranto drove in again, send him in.

"Where do we wait?" Jerry asked as we went back inside.

"The usual places."

"The Garden Room?"

"Why not."

We went to the Garden Room after checking in at the front desk. There were no calls from Jimmy.

I convinced Jerry not to eat again so soon, so we ordered coffee. We were into a second cup each when Artie Muranto walked in. He looked around, saw me and hurried over on his bandy legs.

I moved over so the little cabbie could sit next to me. He eyed Jerry, who was a full foot taller than him.

"The valet said you needed to see me, Eddie. What's up?"

"You picked up a girl a little while ago, a blonde."

"Sure, a chubby girl, right?"

"Right. Can you tell us where you took 'er?"

"I can do better than that," he said. "I can take you there."

Chapter Fifty-Three

Artie didn't drive us there. We followed in the Caddy. When we came to a stop, we saw we were in front of a storage facility.

Jerry and I got out of the car and walked to Artie's cab.

"This is where you left her?" I asked.

"Right here."

"Did you see where she went before you drove away?" Jerry asked.

"Well," he said, rubbing his jaw, "I made a U-turn, but as I drove away, I looked in the rearview mirror."

"And?" I asked.

"She went into one of the buildings."

"Which one?"

Artie thought a moment, looked around at the collection of concrete block buildings, then pointed and said, "That one."

I looked at the building he was pointing to. It had the number "2" on the side of the wall.

"Are you sure?" I asked.

"Yeah," Artie said, then, "no, wait. I was looking in the rearview mirror, so it must've been that one."

He pointed to building 4. Since he wasn't sure, we'd have to check both of them.

"Artie," I asked, "how long ago do you think it was?"

"I logged it." He picked up a book from next to him and leafed through it. "I picked her up at three-twenty-three and dropped her here at three-forty-eight."

I looked at my watch. It was almost five. What were the chances Carol was still there? If she had picked up the money she could've been long gone.

"Okay, Artie," I said, slipping him a sawbuck. "Thanks."

"Anytime, Eddie," he said, and drove off.

Jerry and I turned to face the buildings.

"Maybe we should stay together," Jerry suggested. "After all, I'm armed."

"Good point," I said. "Let's do four first, then two."

"Agreed."

We walked to the door of building four and tried the handle. It was unlocked.

I looked around.

"There's got to be somebody around here," I said. "An attendant, or security."

"Hopefully," Jerry said, "it won't be armed security."

"If there's an office," I added, "it's after five, so they're probably closed."

We entered the building.

"What the hell are we lookin' for?" Jerry asked as we stood just inside the door.

"Maybe we'll get lucky, and Carol will still be here," I said.

"Yeah, right."

"Or maybe we'll find something she left behind."

"Like an empty money bag?" he asked.

"I still don't see how she could've known where the money was."

"Then what the hell was she doin' here?"

"That's what we're gonna try to find out," I said. "But we're gonna need some light."

"I got this," he said, taking a pen-sized flashlight from his jacket pocket. "Until we find some light switches."

"You've got the light, so you lead the way," I said.

"Right."

We moved down the hall. The width of the corrugated metal, roll-down doors indicated the size of the lockers. There were lights in the ceiling, but we hadn't found any wall switches. Maybe they were all on a main breaker. Hopefully there was a light in each locker.

We finished with building four, started for the exit so we could check building two. But on the way back, we saw something we hadn't noticed the first time around. Jerry pointed. One sliding door was open just an inch or so. A dull light showing.

"Might as well check it," I said.

I leaned down, grabbed the bottom of the door and slid it up and open. There was a single, yellow light bulb hanging from the ceiling, getting ready to give out.

The locker was one of the smaller ones, six feet deep, but only about four feet wide. There were boxes along one side, and against the back wall.

"I don't see any empty money bags," Jerry said.

"I can only think of one way Susan would've told Carol about the money."

"Howzat?" Jerry asked.

"If Carol threatened her."

"With what?"

"Cops? Or physical harm?"

"That chubby girl looks like she could kick some ass," he said. "Maybe she did scare the Morrow girl into giving up the money."

"Let's check building two," I said, turning away from the locker.

I heard Jerry start to slide the door shut, and then stop.

"Mr. G.!"

I turned and he pointed into the locker. I moved closer to the door-way so I could see what he was pointing at.

It was a hand.

Chapter Fifty-Four

We moved some boxes until we uncovered the body the hand belonged to. It wasn't Carol, but a man in his thirties.

"Know 'im?" Jerry asked.

"Not a clue."

We went through his pockets, found them empty.

"I don't see any blood," I said. "Any idea how he was killed?"

"From the marks on his neck, I'd say strangled."

"He doesn't look like a very big man."

"Are we thinkin' the chubby blonde did this?" Jerry asked.

"We don't even know if this fella is connected to anythin' we're doin'," I told him.

"A coincidence?" he asked. "I don't think so. That girl came here for a reason."

We both stood up and stared down at the body.

"Maybe to meet him," I said.

"What do you want to do?" he asked.

"Call the police."

"Hargrove?" he asked, with distaste.

"No," I said, "we'll make an anonymous call, then watch for them to identify this fella."

"So you think he's definitely involved in stealin' the St. Jude money."

"We wondered if Susan Morrow had an accomplice," I said. "This guy's young enough to have been a boyfriend."

"A boyfriend who convinced her to steal the money."

"That's what I'm thinkin'," I said. "Come on, let's get out of here and call the cops from a pay phone."

"Hopefully," Jerry said, "nobody saw us, and Artie will keep his mouth shut."

"He will," I assured him.

We left the building, got into the Caddy and drove to the nearest pay phone. Jerry stayed in the car while I made the call.

"And what's your name, sir?" the operator asked after I told her about the body.

I hung up.

When I got back to the car Jerry said, "Done?"

"Done. We can watch from here and see if a car responds."

We could see the storage unit from where we were parked, but a police car wouldn't notice us.

It took twenty minutes, but a patrol car finally pulled through the front gate.

"Twenty minutes," Jerry said, "For a body. That's pretty bad."

"Let's get out of here before the parade starts," I said. "We don't need to see the detectives and medical examiner arrive. Besides, it might be Hargrove."

Jerry started the car and pulled away.

"The Sands?" he asked.

"We might as well," I said. "I don't know where else to look for Carol."

***

When we entered the hotel, one of the desk clerks waved at me.

"Message, Eddie," he said, holding it out.

"Thanks."

"Who from?" Jerry asked.

I read it and refolded it.

"The girls," I said. "They want to talk to us."

"Maybe they wanna confess."

"Wouldn't that come in handy right about now?" I asked.

We took the elevator up and knocked on their door. It was opened by Lisa.

"Just got your message," I said. "What's up?"

She stepped aside to allow us to enter and pointed at the sofa. Jennifer was seated there, with her arm around a distraught Carol.

"She got here about an hour ago and hasn't been able to say much. She just . . . cries."

"We might know why," I said.

We all approached the sofa, and Jennifer looked up at us. Carol kept her head down.

"We just came from the storage unit, Carol," I said. "We found the body."

She looked up at us, surprise and pain on her face.

"Did you kill 'im?" I asked.

She shook her head said, "No. I-I found him that way."

"Did you know him?"

She nodded.

"He came to Vegas after Susan."

"Do you mean he got here second, or he was actually after her?"

"He was after her," she said.

"Was he Susan's accomplice?" I asked.

"She thought he was in love with her. When he came to her with the idea of stealing the money, she agreed,"

"Because she *was* in love with him," I said.

She nodded.

"After such a short time?"

"Susan was vulnerable, Eddie." Carol looked away. "But it was only until she realized all he wanted was the money," she said. "Then she ran, came to Vegas to hide out."

"Which was a bad idea, because he figured she'd come here," Jerry said.

Carol nodded again.

"He knew about Lisa, figured Susan would run here."

"Did he kill 'er, Carol?" I asked.

"He said he didn't."

"And was the money supposed to be in that storage unit?" Jerry asked.

"It was supposed to be," she said. "But apparently it wasn't. Only his body was there."

"How did you come to know him, Carol?" I asked.

"He knew Lisa and Jennifer were Susan's friends," she said. "So he chose to approach me about the money."

"Don't tell me you fell in love with him, too?" I asked.

She glared at me.

"He was nice to me."

Apparently, that was all it took, after all the rejection she had suffered.

"We were gonna share the money," she said. "H-he promised."

I looked at the other girls.

"Let's order some room service," I said, "and we'll talk while we eat."

Carol's head slumped again.

Chapter Fifty-Five

"He approached me on the street one day," she said. "He was . . . charming and handsome. He asked if he could buy me a drink, and after a couple of hours told me who he was. He also told me how much money was involved."

"So, his smile, and the money, did it."

We were all sitting at the bar with our plates of food. Carol had hardly touched hers and I could see Jerry eyeing her French fries.

"Carol," I said, "I think we need to hear the whole story.

"There's not much more to tell," she said. "A day after Susan arrived here, Carlos approached me on the street."

"Carlos?"

She nodded.

"Did Carlos tell you who he was?"

"He said he was Susan's boyfriend," Carol said, "and he was lookin' for her. He asked me if he could buy me a drink so we could talk. I said yes, and we went to a bar."

"Let me guess," I said. "By the time you finished the first drink, you were in love."

She hunched her shoulders.

"You make it sound so stupid," she said.

"What'd he say about Susan?"

"That she ran away from him," she said. "He said she dumped him for no reason, and he wanted to know why. He seemed so . . . sad."

"Did he mention the money?"

"Not then."

"When?"

"The next day."

"You met him again?"

"Yes?"

"Where?"

She hesitated, then said, "We went to a motel."

"Why?" I asked.

"I felt so bad for him," she said. "I wanted to . . . make it better."

"And?"

She hesitated again, then said, "We had sex."

Wow, I thought, that must have really done it for her. An over-weight girl with issues, she would have really fallen for him then.

"And he mentioned the money?"

"Y-yes."

"When?"

"Whatayou mean?"

"I mean before or after?"

"Oh," she said. "After the sex, when we were lying there."

"What did he tell you?"

"That Susan had stolen a lot of money from St. Jude. Originally, he wanted to get it back and return it, but he felt bad that she had dumped him, and now . . ."

"Now what?"

"He said he was thinking about what he and I could do with that money," she said. "Where we could go together."

"And so you went for the idea," Jerry said.

"Y-yes."

"Oh, Carol," Lisa said.

"He was interested in me," she snapped. "He wanted to make me happy. You and Jennifer . . . you haven't been . . . rejected the way I have."

I had the feeling she was talking about more than just being turned away at chorus line auditions. What she was feeling went deeper than that.

"What else?" I asked.

"He wanted me to help him find where Susan was hidin' the money."

"And what did you say?"

"That I'd try, but she was Lisa's friend."

"And?"

"We had a few phone calls after that, and he got mad when I said I couldn't find out anything."

"And then Susan got killed." She nodded, looking miserable.

"Do you think he did it?"

"I-I don't know."

"Why did you go to that storage unit?" I asked.

"I called him from here," she said. "I didn't tell Lisa or Jennifer who I was talking to. H-he told me to meet him there."

"Did he tell you the locker number?"

"Yes."

"Did he say the money was there?" Jerry asked.

"N-no," she answered, "he just said for me to meet him there."

"And what happened when you got there?" I asked.

"N-nothin'," she said. "When I got there I—I found him, already dead."

"What did you do then?"

"I ran," she said. "I came back here."

"Did you look in the locker for the money?" Jerry asked. "Maybe find it and take it?"

"No!" she snapped. "I—I just ran."

Jerry and I exchanged a glance.

"Did-did you call the police?" she asked.

"Yes," I said, "anonymously. We should be hearin' somethin' on the news soon, or in tomorrow's paper. Maybe they'll identify him. Carol, what was Carlos' full name?"

"Dominguez," she said, "he was Carlos Dominguez."

"Dominguez?" I said, looking at Jerry. "Was he related to one of the other St. Jude trustees, Hector Dominguez?"

She nodded.

"He was Hector's son."

Chapter Fifty-Six

It was late, so we told the girls to get some sleep and not to leave the suite for any reason.

"What if there's a fire?" Jennifer asked.

"We'll come and get you," I told her, not sure if she was kidding.

"Did you believe 'er?" Jerry asked.

"Most of it," I said. "Maybe all of it when she admitted how stupid she'd been."

"I heard her say you made it sound so stupid," he said.

"Same thing," I said, as we entered the elevator.

"How can you be sure this body in the locker will be in the newspaper tomorrow?"

I looked at him.

"I'm gonna call the paper," I said.

"That should do it," he admitted. "So whatta we do in the meantime?"

"We're gonna find out if Carlos was Susan's boyfriend, or accomplice, or both."

"How?"

"We're gonna ask his father?"

"We're not goin' to Nashville, are we?" he asked, appalled.

"No," I said, "we'll call 'im."

"Thank God," he said. "I hate country music."

I wasn't fond of it myself.

***

We used an office phone, since I had to make two calls.

"Hector's son is dead?" Danny Thomas asked.

"That's right."

"And it has something to do with Susan and the money?"

"They were both killed in Las Vegas," I said. "That's too much of a coincidence. Plus, Carlos contacted one of Susan's friends and told her about the money."

"What do you want me to do?"

"Give me Hector Dominguez's phone number," I said. "I wanna talk to him."

"Let me get my phone book." I waited and he returned in minutes and gave me the number. "I already told him and Clarence they might hear from you. Are you going to tell him about his son?"

"I'll make up my mind while I'm talkin' to him," I said.

"Anything else, Eddie?"

"Yes," I said, "go home."

"What?"

"Get out of Vegas, Mr. Thomas," I said. "Two people connected to St. Jude are dead, already."

"You think somebody will try to kill me?" he asked, in disbelief.

"I think I want to remove the temptation," I said. "Go home and wait to hear from me."

"All right," he said. "You've convinced me." He hung up.

I broke the connection and dialed the number he gave me. Hector Dominguez answered the phone himself.

"Danny told me I might hear from you," he said. "How can I help?"

"Mr. Dominguez, we've pretty much confirmed that money was stolen from St Jude by Susan Morrow."

"My God, is that what this is about? I can't believe she did that."

I didn't tell him that he had also been a suspect.

"Mr. Dominguez, do you have a son named Carlos?" I asked.

"Yes, I do."

"Do you know where he is?"

"I'm afraid we're not close, since his mother died some ten years ago. Say, why are you asking about my son?"

"It seems he was here in Vegas."

"Oh? Doing what?"

"Looking for Susan. Were you aware they knew each other?"

"No," Dominguez said. "How well?"

"Extremely well, according to him."

"Mr. Gianelli," he said, "what's happened to my son?"

"I'm sorry, sir," I said. "Somebody killed him."

"He and Susan are both dead?"

"Yes."

There was a moment of silence, and then he said, "I see. You think they stole the money together."

"It looks like she came here with the money, and he followed her."

"So, she stole the money, was supposed to share it with him but ran away?"

"I think so."

"Is he the one who killed her?"

"I don't know," I said.

"What do the police say?"

I thought a moment, then said, "They don't confide in me."

"How was he killed? No, never mind—at least his mother's not alive to—is there anything else?"

"No," I said. "I just wanted to find out if you knew about him and Susan."

"Mr. Gianelli . . . will you let me know what happens?"

"Yes, Sir," I said, "I'll let you know."

We both hung up.

"His wife's dead, and now his kid," Jerry said. "Tough luck."

"Yeah," I said, "tough."

Chapter Fifty-Seven

"We have to go back to that locker," I said. "We need to look into all those boxes."

"That won't be easy," Jerry said. "By now it's a crime scene. The cops won't let us in there. They'll have the place covered until they solve the case."

"Maybe we can slip inside," I said.

"We'd have to go and take a look at the situation," Jerry said.

"Okay," I said. "Let's turn in and check the papers in the morning."

"Sounds good," Jerry said. "I could use some shut-eye."

We left the offices and Jerry went up to his suite. I told him I'd spend the night and meet him in the Garden Room at nine.

"The early edition should be out by then," I finished, as the elevator door closed. I took the next one down, thinking I should put in an appearance on the casino floor. As it turned out, I should've gone right to bed.

***

I ran into Buddy Greco in the casino. He was fairly young, about forty, and didn't usually appear in Vegas. As it turned out he told me he was standing in for Tony Martin, who had to cancel.

From 1958 to 1963, Tony Martin had been the highest paid performer in Las Vegas, doing a show at the Desert Inn. After that contract ran out, he took a break. I couldn't blame him. If I was married to Cyd Charisse, I'd want to stay home, too.

My mistake was talking with Buddy too long, because as I turned away from him, I saw Detective Hargrove storming across the casino floor toward me. He had two uniformed policemen on his tail.

"You're under arrest!" he growled.

"What for?"

"I'll figure it out on the way," he said, then turned to the officers and said, "Cuff 'im."

The pit boss on duty was a fella named Harry England. He came walking over, looking concerned.

"Is there anythin' I can do, Eddie?" he asked.

"Yeah!" Hargrove snapped. "Stay out of the way or you'll be next."

"Just let Entratter and Jerry know where I'm goin'," I said.

"Where *are* you goin' " Harry asked.

"To jail," I said. Everybody on the floor watched as they led me away.

***

"You must think I'm a fool," Hargrove said.

"Don't flatter yourself."

He almost came across the table at me. We were in an interrogation room, seated across from each other. His partner, Sanderson, was standing by the door.

"You're not gonna get away with murder, Eddie," he said.

"Is this about that Morrow woman, again?"

"No," Hargrove said, "it's about the guy you strangled and left in a storage locker."

"What the hell are you talkin' about?" I asked. doing my best to act confused.

"Don't fuck with me, Eddie."

"I think I'm the one bein' fucked with, Hargrove," I said. "Who am I supposed to have killed, this time?"

"A man named Carlos Dominguez."

"Never heard of him."

"Maybe this'll jog your memory." He opened a folder and slid a photo of the dead man across the table. It was Carlos Dominguez. I pushed it back.

"Don't know 'im."

"And you still say you never met the dead girl?"

"Right."

He stared at me.

"If you have someone saying different, I'd like to know about it."

Now he glared at me. At the door, Sanderson put his hand to his forehead.

They had nothing.

"Can I get out of here, or do I need a lawyer?" I asked.

Hargrove didn't respond, but Sanderson opened the door.

"Go!" he said.

I thought it was the first word I ever heard him speak.

Chapter Fifty-Eight

As I left the building Jerry was walking up to the door with the lawyer, Kaminsky.

"This giant got me out of bed, and you're walking out?" Kaminsky said.

"Sorry, Kaminsky," I said. "They had nothin' on me."

They both turned and walked to the curb with me, where Jerry had parked the Caddy.

"Just take me home and let me get back to bed," the little lawyer said.

He slept in the backseat as we drove him home, and he stumbled sleepily to his door.

"You dragged him out of bed?"

"He didn't like being woke up," Jerry said. "I had to persuade him to come with me."

"I wonder if I'll need a new lawyer after tonight."

"What did they want with you?"

"Hargrove was trying to pin Dominguez's murder on me."

"Ah," Jerry said, "they i.d.'d him, already."

"Apparently," I said. "Let's go back to the Sands and get some shut-eye. We can decide what to do in the mornin'."

When we got to the elevator Jerry said, "Garden Room at nine?"

I rubbed my face.

"Let's make it nine-thirty."

***

Jerry was seated at a booth when I walked in at nine-forty.

"Sorry I'm late," I said, sliding in across from him.

"It's just ten minutes," he pointed out. "I ordered coffee."

Jerry poured me a cup. The waitress came over and we ordered breakfast.

"So how'd it go last night?"

I told Jerry how Hargrove had showed me a photo of the dead Carlos Dominguez.

"He still wants to pin Susan Morrow's murder on me, while adding the killing of Dominguez. But he's got nothin' to hang me with."

"Unless he realizes we're hidin' the girls."

"We're just keepin' 'em safe," I said.

"Do you still want to get a look inside that locker?" Jerry asked.

"I think we have to," I said. "Have you got any ideas?"

"It depends on how many men they have watchin' it," he said. "If there's more than one it would be a problem."

"But one?"

"One we could handle."

"Without damagin' him?"

"We're talkin' about a cop, Mr. G.," Jerry said. "I'm thinkin' we can take him out without much damage. That is, if we only have one to deal with."

"I guess we better find out."

He pushed his empty plate away and stood up.

***

Hargrove must have left at least one uniformed officer at the scene to keep it secure. There would be another problem, however. The facility was open to the public, and there'd be an employee on duty in the office.

"We should be doin' this at night, when it's dark," Jerry said, as we walked across the lobby.

"Agreed," I said, "but I don't want to waste the day."

But the day wouldn't go to waste. As we approached the front door, Jimmy the valet came rushing in. When he spotted us he waved and ran over.

"We found 'im!"

***

We decided to deal with Willie the Wolf first, and then go and have a look at the locker.

The three of us piled into the Caddy and Jimmy directed us.

Boulder City was originally built in 1931 to house the workers who were building Hoover Dam. Since then, it had undergone many attempts at reclamation until 1960, when it was finally incorporated and Robert N. Broadbent was named the first Mayor.

But some of the old barracks were still standing, although just barely. Jimmy directed us to a building that stood in among others that looked deserted.

"What is it? A hotel?" I asked.

"Not even," Jimmy said. "They rent rooms by the day or week. Lots of the clientele are homeless, and they take a room whenever they accumulate enough cash."

"Willie's in there?" Jerry asked.

"A man matching your description was seen here, yeah," Jimmy said. "When I got the word, I came and took a look. I'm pretty sure it's him."

"Is he still in there?" I asked.

"He was this mornin'," Jimmy said. "I got a man across the street."

Jerry and I looked, as a man waved his arms at us and then pointed to the building.

"Looks like he's there," Jimmy said.

I turned to Jerry.

"Let's have a look."

"Want me to hang around?" Jimmy asked.

"No, you might as well head back to the Sands. I'll let you know if it was him or not. Thanks, Jimmy."

We got out of the car and headed for the building while Jimmy went the other way.

Chapter Fifty-Nine

"How do you wanna play this, Mr. G.?" Jerry asked.

"How do you suggest?"

"I'd play it pretty hard," he answered.

"You know the guy, right?"

"We've met."

"Then you take the lead, Jerry," I said.

"Okay, Mr. G."

Once we got inside, we saw that the place strongly resembled a shooting gallery, where junkies would go to shoot up.

"If Willie's on the needle, he's gonna be a real powderkeg," Jerry said.

"Was he a junkie when you knew him?"

"He dipped his toe in every now and then," Jerry said, looking around, "but nothin' like this."

There were people lying in the hall, half of them clutching pipes or needles.

"I don't see him out here in the hall, but he's supposed to have a room."

"We might as well start knocking on doors," I suggested.

We interrupted various forms of recreation, inspired the ire of some and the embarrassment of others. Finally, we opened a door and found a man lying on a bed, alone. Jerry walked over and looked down at him.

"That's Willie," he said.

I looked around, saw a rifle on a table against the wall. When Jerry turned his head I pointed, and he nodded.

"Okay, Willie," he said, loudly, dropping his big paw on the thin man's chest, "up!"

He closed his hand on the man's shirt and yanked him out of bed. The man's eyes opened just as he hit the floor, face first.

"What the hell—who—hey!" He yelled, rolling over and spitting blood from a split lip.

"Wake up, Willie," Jerry said.

Willie the Wolf's head swiveled back and forth, and he asked, "Who the hell are you guys?"

Jerry grabbed the man again, lifted him onto the bed into a sitting position.

"Hey," Willie said, staring up at Jerry, "don't I know you? From Brooklyn?"

"Yeah, you know me," Jerry said. "And knowin' me, you know you better talk."

"Talk about what?" He looked at me. "Who's this guy?"

"Never mind," Jerry said. "You need to tell me who put the hit out on Howard Hughes."

"What? A hit on Howard Hughes?" His eyes darted around the room. "What are you talkin' about?"

Jerry viciously backhanded Willie across the floor. More blood flew from his mouth, which was now not only cut, but mangled.

"What the fu—"

"I'm gonna ask you one more time," Jerry said, "and then I'm gonna get rough. Who put out the hit on Hughes?"

"If I tell you that, I ain't gonna get any more jobs," Willie said through bloody lips.

"And you ain't gonna get any more jobs if you can't walk," Jerry said. He took his forty-five out which Kaminsky had gotten back from Hargrove and pointed it at Willie's right knee.

"Okay, okay!" Willie screeched. "I'll tell ya."

***

Once we had the name of the man who put out the hit, we made sure Willie knew he wasn't welcome in Las Vegas. We hustled him to the airport, kept his rifle, and bought a ticket on the next plane out. We didn't care where it was going.

"If you come back," Jerry told him, "you won't leave alive. Get it?"

"I get it."

We watched him board the plane, then left the airport.

"Now what?" Jerry asked, as we drove away.

"We need to talk to Entratter," I said. "He'll be able to answer the questions we can't even ask."

***

We found Jack Entratter in his office.

"What is it?" he asked. "I've got a busy morning ahead."

"We found out who put the hit out on Hughes," I told him.

"Oh?" Entratter said. "Who was it?"

"A man named Philip Fontaine."

"Who the hell is that?"

"He works at the Riviera," I said.

"I never heard of him."

"He's only worked there for a few weeks," I said.

"So? Why would he put out a hit on Hughes?"

"He told the hitter that he was acting on the orders of Joey Doves."

"Joey Doves is runnin' the Chicago mob since Momo was deported," Entratter said. "Why would he want Hughes dead?"

"That's our question," I said. "I want to know if Joey Aiuppa really ordered the hit."

"And you want me to ask 'im?"

229

"I could ask 'im," I said. "All I need is a meet."

"You'd have to go to Chicago," Entratter said. "You still have a lot goin' on here. Getting' a flight there, and a flight back, it'd take time."

"Not the flights I'm thinkin' about," I said. "Just set the meet. I'll get there."

Chapter Sixty

When we got to the airport an hour later, Frank Sinatra's Learjet 23, the Christina II, was ready to go. And so was Frank.

Luckily, Frank was still in town, and it only took one phone call to get him to agree to let me use his plane. I hadn't expected him to come along, though, so I was surprised when I boarded to see him there. He was seated on the divan, with a glass of bourbon on a fold out card table in front of him. Frank's fear of flying was well known, and it took a stiff drink or two to ease it long enough for him to fly.

"Where's Big Jerry?" he asked.

"He's stayin' behind," I said. "We're still tryin' to find that St. Jude money."

"You know," he said, "I could give you that money and you could tell Danny Thomas that you found it."

"And I'm sure Danny could replace the money, himself," I said. "That's not the point."

Frank's valet came in and Frank told him, "Let's get goin'."

"Yes, sir."

"You check the weather?"

"Clear all the way to Chicago, Sir."

"Fine."

Frank had his valet check the weather before every flight. Mostly, he took the plane between Vegas, Palm Springs and Los Angeles.

"Have a seat," he said, "and a drink, and tell me what's goin' on. Why Chicago?"

I explained the reason I was going to Chicago.

"Joey Doves," he said. "Why would he want to have Hughes killed?"

"To keep him from buying Las Vegas," I said.

"Why would he care?" Frank asked. "Joey's runnin' Chicago."

"There are two answers to that," I said. "Either he has ambitions that go beyond the Chicago Family, or . . ."

"Or what?"

"Or he never gave the order."

"Then who did?"

"That's another good question."

"You know," Frank said, "whoever gave the order for the hit, I'm kinda sorry they missed."

***

Soon after we took off, Frank picked up a book from nearby. It was called THE DETECTIVE, by Roderick Thorpe.

"Any good?" I asked.

"Very good," he said. "I'm goin' through it a second time. They want me to do it as a movie."

"You've been pretty busy lately," I said.

In '66 both *Cast a Giant Shadow* and *Assault on a Queen* had come out. Frank told me '67 would bring *The Naked Runner* and *Tony Rome*. All four were based on popular books, and *Giant* had him working with John Wayne and Kirk Douglas, although he had not many scenes with them.

"It was impressive to watch them work, though," he said.

In '65 Frank had directed *None But the Brave*, which would be the only film he ever helmed. He took second billing to television's "Cheyenne," Clint Walker. Also, during the filming, actor Brad Dexter had saved Frank from drowning. They became good friends after that. Frank had gotten him a part in *Von Ryan's Express* later that year. I had

232

never met Dexter but knew him for having been one of *The Magnificent Seven* in 1960.

"If I make up my mind in time, they wanna bring *The Detective* out in '68. Then there's another Tony Rome called *The Lady in Cement*. They're tryin' to get Raquel Welch for that one."

I had seen all of Frank's movies and knew that he had recently worked with Virna Lisi and Jill St. John. Raquel Welch was the flavor of the month. Not a very good actress, but what a beauty.

We talked a bit more about Frank's choices in the 60s. It started with *Ocean's 11*, which he loved, but the one he was the most proud of—and I couldn't blame him—was *The Manchurian Candidate*.

'66 had started out good for Frank with his movies plus the recording of his album *Frank Sinatra at the Sands*. He had also recorded his hit record *It Was a Very Good Year* in '65 and won a Grammy for it. '66 brought *That's Life* and *Strangers in the Night*. It was a shame that his 50th year was also the end of the Rat Pack at the Sands, thanks to Howard Hughes.

When we landed at O'Hare, Frank had a car waiting.

"Where's this meeting supposed to take place?" he asked, as we disembarked.

"The Green Door Tavern," I said. The tavern was one of the first buildings erected after the Chicago fire. In the old days, a green door signified a place of a speakeasy.

"On New Orleans Street," Frank said. "Sounds good. Mind if I tag along?"

"I figured that's why you were on the plane when I got there."

We got in the backseat and Frank gave the driver the location. When we arrived, the driver came around and opened the door. As Frank got out, the man leaned over and said something into his ear.

"What was that about?" I asked, as we walked to the door.

"He pointed out that there's a police car across the street with two detectives in it."

"Why doesn't that surprise me."

"Believe me," Frank said, "it doesn't surprise anybody."

We entered the tavern.

Chapter Sixty-One

The Green Door had a back room for private parties. I suppose this qualified. There were two goons covering the door. They patted us down and checked my I.D. before letting us pass.

They didn't bother with Frank's I.D., since everybody in the place knew who he was.

"Joey Doves," Frank said, as we approached the table, "how the hell are you?"

It shouldn't have surprised me that Frank knew Aiuppa.

"Frank," Aiuppa said, "and this is your friend, Eddie G.?"

"This is him."

"Have a seat," Aiuppa said, "I already ordered for all of us."

He was sitting alone at the table, but there were four more men standing around him. We had a seat and a small waiter poured us red wine.

Aiuppa was about sixty, frail and thin but, by all accounts, healthy.

"Eddie," he said, "MoMo spoke very highly of you."

"Glad to hear it," I said. "I guess I should get to the point—"

"Ah, Luigi's here with the food," Aiuppa said, interrupting me. "We can talk after we eat. *Manga*!"

The waiter put a plate of spaghetti and meatballs in front of Frank. Aiuppa obviously knew it was a favorite of his. And because he didn't know me, I got the same. Aiuppa had a large plate of calamari.

"Do you mind if we talk while we eat?" I asked. "I have to get back."

"In such a hurry," Aiuppa said. "Go ahead, talk."

"It's very simple," I said. "Somebody in Vegas put out a hit, using your name."

Aiuppa's eyes went cold. He looked up at one of his men, who simply shook his head.

"Who put the hit out?"

"A man named Philip Fontaine."

Aiuppa put down his fork.

"I don't know 'im," he said. He looked around at his men. "Anybody?"

One man spoke.

"He tried to get a job with us once."

"When?" Aiuppa asked.

"Last year?"

"And?"

"He didn't have the stones," the man said, meaning that Fontaine didn't have the balls for the work.

Now Joey Doves looked at me, while Frank just sat there and ate.

"Who was the target?"

"Howard Hughes."

"*Minchia*!" Aiuppa swore. Frank later told me the word meant "shit." "That's the kind of heat we don't need." He pinned me with a hard stare. "Where is this Fontaine right now?"

"As far as I know he's still in Vegas, at the Riv."

"You did not approach him about this?"

"With all due respect, Don Aiuppa, I wanted to check with you, first."

"And you did the right thing," Aiuppa said. "Go back to Vegas and do nothing about this. It will be handled."

I took that to mean that Philip Fontaine was going to disappear.

Frank knew we had been dismissed and put down his fork.

"Joey," he said, standing.

"Nice to see you, Francis."

Frank put his hand on my shoulder, which I took as my signal to stand.

"Don't worry about those two out front," Aiuppa said, as he picked up his utensils. "They won't bother you."

That was just as well, I didn't want anything to keep us from heading right back to Vegas.

Chapter Sixty-Two

When we got back to McCarran Airport in Vegas, Jerry picked us up. Frank sat in the front seat with him, and they chatted about movies. In the back, I was trying to figure out my next move. The hit on Howard Hughes had been neutralized on two counts. Both Willie the Wolf and Philip Fontaine were going to disappear. I wasn't sure why Fontaine had tried to put out a hit and blame it on Joey Doves, but I was sure Joey was going to find out. It might have been revenge for not hiring him, or maybe Fontaine was trying to save the Riv from Hughes. But whatever the reason, I could stop thinking about it for now. Jerry and I were still looking for the St. Jude money, and, at the same time, maybe we'd find out who killed Susan and her boyfriend, Dominguez.

When we got to Vegas, Frank told Jerry to drop him at Caesars Palace, not the Sands. Then looked at both of us and said, "Don't ask."

We didn't.

Jerry drove us to the Sands, and during the ride brought me up to date on what had happened since I left.

"Nothin'!"

"Not a thing?"

"Your shamus buddy's man is still watchin' the girls like a hawk. He ain't gonna let another one slip away."

"And?"

"Maheu came lookin' for you, wanted an update on the hit," Jerry said. "I told him you were in Chicago."

"I better call and tell him the hit's off."

"Is it?" Jerry asked.

"Joey Doves is gonna take care of it himself," I said.

"And you believe he had nothin' to do with it?"

"I did believe him at the time," I said, "but even if he was lyin', he's callin' it off now. He doesn't want to be linked to a hit on Howard Hughes."

"I don't blame 'im," Jerry said. "That'd bring a helluva lot of heat."

I had pretty much the same conversation with Entratter later, but that was after I called Maheu and gave him the news.

***

"How did it go in Chicago?" Entratter asked. We were sitting in his office. "I assume you were meeting with Joey Doves. Why else would you go?"

"You're right," I said. "The hit's off. Jerry and I took care of the third-rate hit man ourselves, and Aiuppa is takin' care of the man who ordered it."

"Good," Entratter said. "I know killin' Hughes would bring a lot of heat, but it would also have solved a lot of problems."

"It could still happen," I said, "but not today, and not in Vegas."

"You may be right," Entratter said. "What about the St. Jude thing?"

"Still workin' on it," I said, "but I sent Danny Thomas home, just to be on the safe side."

"Good," Entratter said. "What's your next stop?"

"We have an idea where the money might be," I said. "We just have to take a look."

"Well, do it, man," Entratter said. "I need you back here. I'm still runnin' a business . . . for now."

"Right."

Jerry and I left Entratter's office. With Frank, Dino and the Rat Pack's days at the Sands coming to an end, Jack's last day might not be far behind, either. After that I'd have to decide what I was going to do—that is, if the decision was left up to me.

"The storage unit?" Jerry asked, as we took the elevator down.

"There's only one reason for that storage facility to be involved," I said.

"If the money's there."

"Yes."

"Then we have to figure out a way to have a look. But . . ."

"But what?" I asked.

"What do you think Hargrove would do it he found three-hundred-thousand dollars?"

We both knew the answer to that.

Chapter Sixty-Three

There was one uniformed cop on the front door of storage facility four.

"Oh, this is gonna be easy," Jerry whispered.

We had parked down the block and walked the rest of the way.

"Unless there's another man inside."

"I don't see why there would be," Jerry said. "There ain't another door."

"So what do we do?"

"He paces back and forth," Jerry said, "then sits a while, then starts again."

"So? We take him while he's seated?"

"No," Jerry said, "while he's pacing. He walks from one side to the other. I'll wait at this end and take him out."

"But not kill him," I said.

"No," he said, "I don't kill cops, Mr. G."

"Good to know."

"You wait here," he said. "You'll see when I take him out."

"Gotcha."

When the cop was pacing the other way, his back momentarily to us, Jerry closed the distance to the building, pressed his back against the wall around the corner. The cop turned, came back toward us, and as he got to the end of the building, turned again to return to his seat. Jerry stepped out, wrapped his arm around the man's neck, and in seconds lowered him to the ground. Then he waved at me, and I trotted over to him.

"He'll be out for a while," he said. "Come on."

We entered the building and made our way to the storage locker we had found Dominguez's body in. The corrugated metal door was half-way. Jerry slid it up the rest of the way and we went in. Once again, we only had Jerry's pen-light to work with. There was a blub in the ceiling, but somebody had smashed it. I hadn't noticed that the first time.

"Okay," I said, pointing, "that's where we found him."

"No blood," Jerry said. "He was strangled.

"He was a strong, young man," I pointed out. "It had to be some-body stronger."

"If you grab someone from behind, and exert the right pressure, that's not necessarily true."

"So it had to be somebody who knew what they were doin'."

"Right."

I looked around at the boxes. They were all shapes and sizes, some dark brown, others that had obviously been scored from grocery or liq-uor stores. Some had been opened, others were still sealed.

"These sealed boxes," I pointed out, "maybe somebody found what they were lookin' for and didn't look any further."

"If somebody found that St. Jude money," Jerry said, "it's long gone."

"If Hargrove found it, and decided to keep it, he had to hide it some-where else."

"And if Susan and Dominguez had another partner, maybe he's got it, and is long gone," Jerry offered.

"Well," I said, "we've got an unconscious cop outside, so we better take advantage and have a look around."

"Right."

We went through the open boxes first, and then started slitting the tape on the sealed ones.

"Most of this is junk," Jerry said. "Why do people keep broken radios and T.V.'s, old clothes, out of date calendars—"

"Do you know what we're not findin'?" I asked.

"Money?"

"Anythin' personal," I said. "There are no photos, or personal papers."

"Yeah, I noticed that," Jerry said. He looked around. "You think this is a fake?"

"All this junk is to make it look like it's somebody's storage unit, but it was probably only used to hide the money."

"But there's no money here now," Jerry said. "It's gone."

We stood there and looked around.

"We have to get out of here before that cop wakes up," I said.

Jerry looked at his watch.

"We've got a few minutes, but we better go just to make sure."

We left the locker, went to the front door and cracked it to take a look. The cop was still out.

"Let's go," I said.

We slipped out, stepped over him and hotfooted it to the Caddy. Once we were seated, we relaxed.

"Okay," I said, "we agree the money had to have been there, but now it's gone."

"So we're nowhere."

"The money had to have been taken by somebody who knew it was here."

"Only the people we know were involved are dead," Jerry said.

"If we forget about Hargrove, who's that leave us?" I asked.

"The three girls?"

"I'm afraid so."

Chapter Sixty-Four

When we got back to the Sands, we sat in the dark parking lot for a few moments.

"So, what you're saying' is it's one or more of the girls," Jerry said.

"I've been thinkin'," I said. "I think it's Lisa, Jennifer, or both of them."

"Not the chubby blonde?"

"No, not Carol," I said. "I think Dominguez got over on her, and she's not as tough as she makes out. In fact, I think it's Lisa, or it's Lisa *and* Jen."

"So you think the Morrow girl blabbed about the money to her friend, Lisa."

"That seems likely."

"So, you think Lisa told Jennifer, and then they killed Susan? Who killed Dominguez?"

"I'm still trying to sort this out," I said. "We know somebody was after Susan, because they came after me. So whoever that was probably killed her. But they didn't get the money, so they went to the apartment to question the roommates."

"That's where I came in."

"Right," I said. "You killed them, and we brought the girls here."

"So if they knew where the money was, we kept them from getting to it."

"And if it was in the storage unit, they killed Dominguez and got to it."

"After he called the chubby girl. And then she found him."

"Carol, right."

He snapped his fingers.

"Why can't I ever remember her name?"

"Maybe because you like chubby girls, and that's what you remember."

"Yeah," Jerry said, "I do like chubby girls. I'd be real happy if this one wasn't a killer."

I shifted uncomfortably.

"We better turn in. We can work on the girls tomorrow."

"Work on 'em how?"

"Hopefully," I said, "I'll know that by the time I wake up."

We left the Caddy and went into the Sands. As I got off the elevator on my floor Jerry asked, "Breakfast in the mornin'?"

"Why not?" I said, and the door closed.

***

I woke the next morning without a clue. How were we supposed to prove the girls had the money? If we let them go, they might lead us to it, but they might also get killed. There was still a killer out there, presumably responsible for the deaths of both Susan Morrow and her boyfriend. If they didn't have the money, they were still looking for it, like we were. But unlike us, they were willing to kill for it.

Of course, we could've turned the girls over to Detective Hargrove, and let him take it from there. But I disliked Hargrove too much to help him solve his case.

I showered, got dressed and went down to meet Jerry for breakfast. When the elevator door opened, Dean was there, dressed in his golf yellows and plaids.

"Where are your clubs?" I asked.

"Already at the course," he said. "Frank told me about your meet with Aiuppa. I gotta say, you've got balls, Eddie."

"You might put that another way and say I don't have any brains," he said.

"Well, we both know that ain't true, Pally."

I changed the subject.

"It looks like Frank's signing with Caesar's Palace," I said.

"Howard Hughes didn't leave him much choice," Dino said.

"What about you?"

"I'm talking with the Riviera."

"Then it really is the end of an era in Las Vegas."

"Had to happen sometime," Dean said. "But it was fun while it lasted. Actually, I'm too busy to put in as much time here as I used to. My show is number one, I've got movies to make and albums to record. And then there's golf." He shrugged. "Life goes on."

I knew Dean's recording career was soaring. He had knocked the Beatles off the number one spot on the charts with *"Everybody Loves Somebody."* And his variety show was a hit from the very first episodes. And his two Matt Helm movies, *The Silencers* and *Murderers' Row*, had been major hits.

When the elevator door opened, we stepped into the lobby.

"I'm havin' breakfast with Jerry in the Garden Room," I said, "Care to join us."

"I'll have somethin' at the club," Dino said. "Besides, I'm sure you two have business to discuss."

"Yeah, we do."

As we separated, he called out, "Hey, Pally."

"Yeah?"

"Remember," he said, "you're a smart man, Clyde. A smart man."

"Thanks, Dino."

Chapter Sixty-Five

At breakfast, Jerry and I brainstormed and decided to approach the girls directly. It was the only thing left to do. The only other thing that could help was if whoever killed Susan Morrow tried to kill us, and we caught him.

We left the Garden Room and headed for the elevator. Along the way we ran into Danny.

"I sent my man home for a while, thought I'd take over," he said. "Where are you headed?"

"To talk to the girls," I said. "We're thinkin' they know where the money is."

"Want me to come along?"

"To talk to three young women?" I asked. "Penny would love that. Why don't you just take off. I think Jerry and I can handle it from here."

"Okay," he said. He started to walk away, then turned. "Oh, the boyfriend thing?"

"Susan Morrow's boyfriend?" I asked. "Dominguez, right? The kid?"

"No," he said. "She didn't have a boyfriend."

"What?"

"That's the word I got."

"Are you sure?"

"Pretty sure, yeah."

"Okay, Danny, thanks."

Jerry and I got into the elevator.

"If the kid wasn't her boyfriend, what was he doin' in Vegas? How did he know about the money?"

"If he's not connected to her, he's connected to somebody."

"His father?"

I nodded.

"So, two of the three people Danny Thomas hired to run his hospital stole from it?"

"That's what it looks like."

"Jesus," he said, "that's gonna crush him."

"He'll have to get over it and look hard at his next choices," I pointed out.

We walked to the girls' suite and knocked. Lisa answered.

"Any news?" she asked.

"Lots," I said. "Can we come in?"

She nodded and backed up. As we entered Jennifer looked over from the bar, and Carol from the sofa. She still looked crestfallen.

"We need to have a talk, ladies," I said.

"About what?" Jennifer asked.

"Money."

Carol looked up.

"You found it?"

"No," I said.

"Have you found out who killed Carlos?" Carol asked.

"No, not that, either," I said. "But we found out he wasn't Susan's boyfriend."

"He wasn't?" Carol asked. "But he said—"

"He told you that to get you to play along with him," I said. "He was hoping one of you three could help him find the money, and he chose you, Carol."

"Because I was the dumbest?" she asked, bitterly.

"Not dumb," Jerry said.

"Maybe just the easiest to get to," I offered.

"Carol never knew where the money was," Lisa said.

"None of us did," Jennifer added.

"Well, Carol didn't," I said. "That I believe."

"What do you mean?" Lisa asked. "You think we do?"

"Jerry and I have come to the conclusion that you and Jennifer are not as innocent as you make out."

"Why would you say that?" Jennifer asked.

"Because," I said, "it's the only thing that makes any sense. You either have the money or you know where it is."

"And if we have it," Lisa asked, "just where is it?"

"It could be right here in this suite," I said.

"How?" she asked. "You rushed us out of our apartment without so much as an overnight bag."

"That's right, we did," I said. "We brought you here to protect you, but I don't think we can keep you here any longer."

"B-but," Carol said, "whoever killed Susan and Carlos is still out there."

"Yes," I said, "they are. You girls better pack whatever clothes you have here, and head back to your apartment."

"B-but you can't put us out!" Carol complained. "We'll be killed."

"Shut up, Carol!" Lisa snapped. She used a voice and displayed a manner I hadn't seen before.

"What about you, Lisa?" I asked. "Aren't you afraid you'll be killed?"

She folded her arms.

"If you thought we were in danger you wouldn't let us go," she said, confidently.

"Well, then," I said, "be out within the hour. The maids will be in here to clean."

"But Eddie—" Jennifer stared but was silenced by Lisa.

"Shut up, Jen!" Lisa snapped.

Jennifer fell silent. It was clear now who was in charge.

"Lisa," I said, "let's talk in the bedroom."

Lisa looked at Jennifer and Carol.

"Don't say anything until I get back," she told them.

Jennifer went over and sat next to Carol. Jerry walked to the bar and sat on a stool. I followed Lisa to the bedroom and closed the door. She turned to face me, her arms folded.

"What's going on, Eddie?" she demanded.

"I feel like a fool," I said. "I've been playin' protector to the pretty girls, while the pretty girls have been playin' me—and Jerry—for fools."

"Have we?"

"You know you have," I said. "At least, you and Jennifer have."

"A smart man like you?" she asked. "Played for a fool by a couple of showgirls?"

"Don't rub it in, Lisa," I said. "Now where's the money?"

"I don't know where the money is."

"Who killed Susan?"

"I don't know that, either."

"But you knew about the money."

"Susan told me," she said. "She said she stole the money from St. Jude over a period of time."

"Did she say she had help?"

"Yes."

"Who?"

"That she didn't say," Lisa answered. "But she said when it got to three hundred thousand dollars, she panicked."

"And came here?"

"Yes," she replied. "She said somebody was after her for the money."

"And she was right," I said. "And now they're after you."

"You're putting us out on the street," she said, "so I guess we'll have to handle that on our own."

"And what about Carol?"

"Carol got herself involved by falling for Carlos," she said.

"And you have no idea who killed him," I said.

She shrugged.

"For all I know, Carol did it."

"I don't think so," I said.

"Why not?"

"She's the only one I don't think was playin' me and Jerry," I said. "She really fell for Dominguez."

"And maybe she found out he was playing *her*, so she killed him."

"So you'd hang her out to dry to save yourself and Jennifer?"

"I'm just saying," she said.

Chapter Sixty-Six

As we came out of the bedroom I said, "We better get goin', Jerry."

"Right, Mr. G."

Lisa went over to stand next to Jennifer and Carol, who were still seated on the sofa.

"Thanks for keeping us safe this long, boys," Lisa said.

"Sure," I said. "Good luck."

Jerry and I left the suite.

"Are we really puttin' them out?" Jerry asked.

"Yes," I said, "but we'll keep an eye on them."

"In case somebody tries to kill them?"

"Or in case they lead us to the money."

When we got to the lobby, Danny was still there, looking like he was waiting for us.

"What's up?" I asked.

"I thought twice about leavin'," Danny said. "Thought you might need me."

"We're lettin' the girls go, and I want to tail them," I said.

"Well," he said, "there's three of 'em and they might split up, so maybe it's a good thing I stayed."

"You're probably right," I said, "but I really wanted you to look a little deeper at Hector Dominguez."

"The father of the dead kid?"

"You said he wasn't her boyfriend," I said. "Then why was he here?"

"You think the father sent 'im?" Danny asked.

"I think I was all wrong when we started, and I thought these girls were wide-eyed innocents. So maybe we were wrong when we cleared those other two in Nashville."

"But you don't suspect 'em both," Danny said.

"No," I said, "just Dominguez, otherwise what was his kid doin' here?"

"Okay," Danny said, "I'll get one of my guys to switch places with me, and I'll check it out."

"Okay, great," I said. "Thanks, Danny."

"You got it," he said, "but for now, who should I take if and when they split?"

"You take Carol," I said. "I don't think she's involved, but I could be wrong again." I looked at Jerry. "You take Jennifer, and I'll take Lisa."

"Who gets the Caddy?" he asked.

"You take it," I said. "They'll have to use cabs from here, so I'll use one, too."

"Okay."

"We better get out of sight, for now," I said. "They could be comin' down right behind us."

They did come down, but they came down one-by-one, instead of leaving the building together, and then splitting up.

We had taken cover, so as Jennifer appeared first, Jerry started after her. A few moments later, Carol came out of the elevator.

"See ya later," Danny said, and went after her.

That left me waiting for Lisa. When she didn't appear, I hurried to the desk.

"What's up Eddie?" the female clerk asked. Her name tag said: BECKY.

"I wanna check suite seven-fourteen for outgoing calls, Becky.

"Sure thing, Eddie." She hit some buttons. "Looks like they're on a call right now."

"Any way we can listen in?"

"At the beginning of the call, yeah. If I click in now, they'll hear it."

"I see."

"It doesn't matter, though," she said. "They just ended the call."

"Thanks, Becky."

I got back to my corner just in time to see the elevator doors open and Lisa step out. She walked hurriedly across the lobby to the front door. I quickly stepped in after her. I watched through the glass door while she got a cab from a valet. As the cab pulled away, I hurried out and said, "Cab! Quick!"

"Right, Eddie."

He waved and a taxi pulled up. I jumped in.

"Follow that cab that just pulled out," I instructed.

The driver turned and grinned. It was Artie Muranto. I hadn't even noticed it was a Blue Flamingo cab.

"You got it, boss."

"Artie!"

"That was one of our cabs," he said, pulling away. "It wouldn't be hard to find out where it went without actually followin' it. I mean, if you don't wanna get caught."

"Not a bad idea," I said, "but I want to be right on them, for now."

"Okay, boss," Artie said. "Whatever you want."

I could see the Blue Flamingo colored cab a few cars ahead of us. I hoped it was the right one, as there were quite a few on the road.

"Don't worry, Mr. G.," Artie said, as if reading my mind, "that's him."

"Just don't lose 'im."

Chapter Sixty-Seven

Halfway through the ride I had an idea of where she was going.

"Don't get too close," I said. "I'm pretty sure I know her destination."

"You got it!"

Eventually, she proved me right by pulling up in front of the building where the three girls lived. She was going home.

"Stop here."

Artie pulled to the curb right away. We watched as Lisa got out of his cab and entered her building.

"Wait here," I said.

"Meter runnin'?" he asked.

"Of course."

I got out and trotted to her building, but didn't go in. I looked into the lobby from outside, and only saw the doorman, Vincent. I opened the door and went inside.

"Hey, Eddie," he said. "My girl loved the show and dinner the other night. I impressed her with who I know."

I had left two tickets for Vincent at the door, for whenever he wanted to use them. The same for dinner.

"Glad to hear it, Vincent," I said. "Listen, I was tryin' to catch up to Lisa. Can I go up?"

"You could," he said, "but she ain't up there."

"I saw her come in—"

"Oh, she came in," he said, "But she didn't go up."

"Where'd she go?" I was afraid she'd used a back door to lose me.

"Down," he said, turning his thumb down. "Every apartment has a storage unit in the basement. Go ahead."

"Thanks, Vincent."

I went to the elevators and waited for one, then took it to the basement. When I stepped out it was dimly lit, but I could see a word painted on the concrete wall with an arrow pointing. It said: STORAGE.

I followed the hallway to a chain link door, which was ajar. I could hear someone moving. I opened the door wide and entered. On both sides of me were units of differing sizes and shapes, all behind chain link doors. I kept moving until I saw one door that was open. When I reached it I looked inside and saw Lisa leaning over an open box.

"So the money was here all the time," I said.

She turned quickly and stared at me, then stood up.

"When Susan arrived, we hid it down here," she said. "When you and Jerry came to our rescue, we had no time to move it."

"You, Jennifer and Susan?" I asked. "What about Carol?"

"Naw," she said, "we knew we couldn't trust Carol. Then when that fella, Carlos, came to town, she proved it."

I looked past her at the open carton.

"Is it all there?"

"Oh, yeah," she said, "it is. Half for you, half for me."

"And what about Jennifer?" I asked. "And your other partners?"

"Partners?"

"You know," I said, "whoever killed Susan and Carlos. That is, unless you did it."

"No," she said, "I didn't kill them."

"Then who did?"

From behind me a man's voice said, "I did."

I turned and saw a middle-aged man pointing a gun at me.

"Let me guess," I said. "Hector Dominguez."

"Very good, Mr. Gianelli," he said.

"You killed Susan?" Lisa asked.

"I did," Dominguez said. "She wouldn't tell me what she did with the money."

"Why should she?" I asked.

"Because we stole it together," Dominguez said. "That is, she stole it after I showed her how."

"And Carlos?" I asked. "You killed your own son?"

"He was no son of mine," he spat. "Step-son several times removed. Fourth or fifth wife. I forget. In any case, he figured out what I was planning and tried to warn Susan. I had to take care of him."

"But why kill her before she could tell you where the money was?" I asked.

"Ah, well," he said, "she was very stubborn, she struggled, and . . ." He shrugged.

"So it was an accident."

"Pretty much."

"But Carlos wasn't."

"No," he said, "he had to go."

Dominguez was a large man, with big hands. Danny Thomas had told me the man was a surgeon. I couldn't imagine he was a good one, not with paws that big.

I looked at Lisa. She was good. I still couldn't tell if Dominguez's appearance surprised her, or if she had called him. My guess was she had called him from the Sands and arranged to meet him here. But why? Why split the money with him?

I wanted to keep Dominguez talking, because if he was talking to me, he wasn't pulling the trigger.

"Okay," I asked, "how did you get Susan to agree to steal the money?"

"I can answer that," Lisa said. "Susan always had a thing for older, professional men."

"She was lost," Dominguez said, "always looking for daddy."

"And daddy got her to embezzle three hundred grand."

"She was happy to do it," he said.

"At first," Lisa said. "She was scared when she came here."

"Of what?" I asked, then looked at Dominguez, "you?"

"She got cold feet," he said, "but it was after we got to three-hundred-thousand. I told her to calm down, but before I knew it, she was gone."

"With the money."

"Right."

"How did you track her here?"

"She mentioned her friend, Lisa, who lived in Vegas. Since that was the only friend she ever talked about, I took a shot."

"And sent some goons," I said.

"Well," Dominguez said, "I didn't expect *your* goon to kill them."

"I thought you were supposed to be a surgeon."

He smiled.

"That's what everybody is supposed to think."

"Including Danny Thomas?"

"I like Danny," Dominguez said, "but the truth is, he let the fox into the henhouse and didn't know it."

"So now what?" I asked. "You two split the money?"

"Oh no," Dominguez said, "I've gone through too much to share."

"Wait a minute," Lisa said. "I called you—"

"So what?"

Suddenly, she looked scared.

"You said you'd help me—"

"Shut up!" he shouted. "Now, both of you, come out of there." He gestured with the gun. It looked like all the talking might be done, even though I still had a few questions.

Chapter Sixty-Eight

"Seems like you had a lot of help along the way," I said. "Now you're alone."

"Don't worry about me," he said. "Lisa, lock it up."

She closed the chain link door and locked it.

"The key, please," he said, holding out his left hand.

She handed it to him.

"Now what?" I asked. "You gonna walk us past the doorman at gunpoint?"

"The doorman's taking a little nap," he said. "How do you think I got in here?"

"You killed Vincent?" Lisa blurted.

"I said nap, girl," Dominguez said. "I don't kill anyone unless I have to."

"Or by accident," I added.

"I told you," he said, "she struggled. It wasn't my fault. Now let's walk to the elevator."

"Eddie," Lisa bleated, "you're supposed to be keeping us safe. See what happens when you put us out on our own?"

"Hey," I said, "*you* called him."

We walked ahead of Dominguez toward the elevator. I was hoping the door would open and someone would step out—Jerry, preferably, but anyone would have done. I doubted Dominguez would shoot a stranger, and it might have given Lisa and me a chance to escape.

But we reached the elevator without it opening, so that chance didn't appear.

"Press the button," Dominguez instructed. "Let's go!"

When the door opened and revealed an empty interior, Dominguez yelled, "Move!"

I had no way of knowing how comfortable this man was with fire-arms. Jerry had once told me that people unfamiliar with guns were fairly easy to disarm. He'd tried to show me, but I had been a poor pupil. I wasn't about to try it now.

"Against the wall," he said.

It was a small elevator. Lisa and I flattened our backs on one side, while Dominguez stood against the other and pressed the button for the main floor.

When we got off and walked toward the door, I could see Vincent's body lying on the floor behind his desk. I couldn't tell whether or not he was breathing.

We went through the front door and out on the street. Dominguez put the gun, a small revolver, into his pocket and kept his hand there.

"Which way?" I asked.

"Turn right," Dominguez ordered. "I'll tell you when to stop."

"You're takin' a chance," I pointed out, "leaving the money in that locker."

"Not really," he said. "I have the key. Now I just need to take care of the two of you."

I looked around for something—anything—helpful, but all I saw were people walking by, cars on the street. We could've made a break for it, forcing him to shoot out in the open, but I'd be taking a chance with Lisa's life. If it was just me, I would've ran out into traffic—even though there wasn't much of it at the moment.

"The blue Plymouth," Dominguez said.

No way we could get into that car. If we did, we were dead.

I stopped and turned.

"No."

"What?" he said.

"If you want to kill us, do it here and now," I said. "We're not gettin' into your car."

"Don't be stupid," he said, looking around. "Get in the car."

I looked at Lisa. As frightened as she was, she jumped on board.

"No, Eddie's right," Lisa said. "Either shoot us here, or let us go."

As he narrowed his eyes, his hand started to come out of his pocket.

Chapter Sixty-Nine

He stopped just short of clearing his pocket with the gun, clearly still having second thoughts. I decided to play on that, if I could.

"So," I asked, "what's it gonna be?"

"You're forcing my hand," he said.

"How did you get into this, Dominguez?" I asked. "You're supposed to be a respected surgeon."

"My hands aren't what they used to be," he said. "They shake too much."

That was when I noticed the tremor in his left hand.

"In times of stress, right?" I said.

He shook his head and jammed his right hand deep into his pocket, again.

"I can shoot you through my pocket," he said, "and be gone in seconds."

"Both of us?" I asked. "One shot? And be sure we're dead without checking our bodies? I think that would take several seconds. Enough time for somebody to see you."

He looked around frantically. Pedestrian traffic was light, but there were some people on both sides of the street. He was starting to lose it.

"You should've shot us in that basement," I said. "That's what an experienced criminal would've done."

He thought about that for a moment, then gritted his teeth and started bringing the gun out. We were six feet apart and I moved, trying to close the distance between us before the gun came out.

His eyes went wide as he saw me coming and tried to bring the gun to bear. I tackled him around the waist, causing him to pull the trigger once as we went down to the ground. We rolled around on the concrete for a few moments until, being younger and stronger, I was able to take the advantage. I pinned him to the ground and disarmed him. I got to my feet with his gun and backed away. Looking around for Lisa, fearing she might have been hit by his stray bullet. I saw her crouched against the front of a building.

"Are you all right?" I asked.

Shakily, she got to her feet.

"I—I think so."

I looked around to see if anyone else might have been hit, but there were no casualties. Dominguez was still on the ground, curled into a ball. The realization had hit him that it was all over.

"Now what?" Lisa asked.

"Now we call the police."

"But—" she grabbed my arm. "—the money."

"The money goes back to St. Jude, Lisa."

"W-what will happen to us?" she asked.

"I don't know," I said. "You and Jen knew where the money was. I can say you took me to it, intending to turn it in."

"Y-you'd do that?"

"I told you I'd protect you, didn't I?" I reminded her. "Let's get back to your building, see how Vincent is, and use the phone."

***

Vincent was alive, but still unconscious when we got there. He had a deep scalp wound from where Dominguez had struck him with his pistol.

I pushed Dominguez into a corner, covered him with his own gun in one hand, and picked up the phone. I made the call I hated to make.

"Yeah, police?" I said. "I need to speak to Detective Hargrove." I listened for a second and then said, "Who's callin'? Tell 'im it's his worst nightmare."

Chapter Seventy

Smoke was shooting from Hargrove's ears as he entered the lobby. By the time he arrived, two uniformed officers had responded, along with an ambulance for Vincent who, with his head bandaged, was led past the detective as he entered,

"This better be good," he said to me.

"I'm gonna give you the killer and the missing money. Is that good enough for you?"

Over his shoulder I could see his partner's eyebrows shoot up.

"Go ahead," Hargrove said, "I'm listening."

I told him about Dominguez urging Susan Morrow to steal from St. Jude, and how—when the amount got high enough—she panicked and ran.

"He came lookin' for her and, while tryin' to force her to tell him where the money was, accidently killed her. He then hired some thugs to scare me off and find the money."

"Only your buddy Jerry knocked 'em off."

"Right. Meanwhile Dominguez's step-son—former step-son—tried to step in to help Susan, and was killed, as well."

"Mr. Dominguez?"

"Yes."

"He killed his own son?"

"Former step-son, apparently several wives back," I said.

"And where's the money?"

"In a storage locker in the basement."

Hargrove looked at Lisa.

"And what about her and her girlfriends?"

"She brought me here to show me where the money was," I said. "Before we could get to it, Dominguez showed up with a gun."

Hargrove turned to his partner and said, "Hook him up and watch him," pointing at Dominguez. To me he said, "Show me the money."

"He's got the key," I said.

Hargrove went through Dominguez's pocket, retrieved the key, and then followed us down to the locker.

Once he saw the stacks of money in the box, he turned and said to Lisa, "You knew it was here all along?"

She froze and I answered, "She suspected it might be here, she had given Lisa a key to store her things when she got here, but she didn't know who to trust."

"So, she finally decided to trust you, huh?"

"That's right."

"It better all be here."

"I'm sure you'll get every penny of it back to Danny Thomas for St. Jude," I said.

"You'll both have to come to headquarters with me and make statements," Hargrove said. "Then you can go. I'll put the money in our property room for safekeeping."

"I'll notify Danny Thomas that the money has been recovered," I said. "I'm sure he'll be very pleased."

Hargrove looked down at the money with what I could only describe as a hungry look, and then closed the box.

***

I sat alone in an interrogation room while they typed up my statement. When the door finally opened it was Sanderson who came in. He placed my statement on the table along with a pen.

"Sign it, and you can go," he said.

"Where's Lisa?"

"She's doing the same thing."

I read the statement quickly, found it accurate, and signed it.

"You can go," Sanderson said, picking it up.

"What about Dominguez?" I asked, standing. "Has he confessed?"

"Hargrove is still working on him," Sanderson said. "It must have really burned your butt to give him this collar."

"Actually," I said, "I wanted to give it to you.'

"Why didn't you?"

I smiled.

"I couldn't remember your name."

He frowned as I left the room.

***

I found Lisa waiting out on the front steps.

"We better get goin' before Hargrove changes his mind," I said.

"Should we get a cab?" she asked.

"No need," I said, inclining my head toward the curb. She turned her head and saw Jerry sitting in the Caddy.

"How did he know we were here?"

"I called him," I said. Actually, "I called the Sands and left a message for him. He should know where Jen and Carol are. Come on."

When we got into the Caddy, Jerry said, "The Sands?"

I looked at Lisa.

"I think I want to go home," she said.

"Take the lady home, Jerry."

He pulled away from the curb.

***

Lisa identified the relief doorman, who was now working full shifts until Vincent recovered. We watched her get into the elevator and then left.

"You think she woulda thanked you for savin' her life," Jerry said.

"I also kept her from gettin' the money," I reminded him. "I don't think she's ready to thank me for that."

We got into the car and headed back to the Sands.

"Where did the other girls go?" I asked.

"They just led us away from their building," Jerry said. "By the time I realized what they were doin', it was too late to get back and help you. I'm sorry, Mr. G."

"Don't be," I said. "It all worked out."

"And what's left for us to do?"

"Not much," I said. "The money is going back to St. Jude, so Danny Thomas is happy. The killer's been found and arrested. The hitman's been neutralized, so Howard Hughes is in no danger. And Hughes is still buying Vegas properties."

"There's no way to stop 'im?" Jerry asked.

"I don't know if even Frank and Dino are still tryin'," I said. "Things are changin' in Vegas, Jerry. Things are changin' a lot."

Epilogue

Between 1966 and '68, Howard Hughes bought The Castaways, the New Frontier, the Landmark Hotel and Casino, the Silver Slipper and, of course, the Sands. Vegas continued to change after that, with the mob moving out. Frank moved his act to Caesar's Palace, while Dino went to the Riviera. Sammy performed at several Vegas locations, such as the Frontier, but eventually refused to perform anywhere that would not let black performers stay in their rooms. He eventually became a top headliner, remaining friends with Frank and Dino, and forming a close relationship with Elvis Presley.

Vegas continued to change over the years, even undergoing an attempt to make it a family destination. Frank and Dino would have shuddered to see what had become of the Rat Pack's former haunt. I know I did.

***

After Jacqueline's Thanksgiving dinner, we got into her car and drove to my building.

"I'm sorry," she said.

"For what?"

"I blindsided you, and you had to answer questions all night."

"Believe me," I told her, "I like reminiscing about the guys."

We pulled up in front of my building and her driver got out and came around to open the car door.

"Goodnight, Eddie," she said.

"Jacqueline."

She kissed my cheek and I got out.

Riding up in the elevator, I thought more about the "old days." It didn't take long for Jack Entratter to leave the Sands rather than work for Howard Hughes. The same thing happened with Robert Maheu, who parted ways with Hughes in 1970, and had nothing but bad things to say about him.

When I got into my apartment, I sat on the sofa, worn out from the night's activities. I wasn't even sure I could make it to bed.

1967 was pretty much the end of the Rat Pack's Vegas. Frank and Dino's friendship endured over the ensuing years, but their time on a Vegas stage together waned. There were so many more stories in my head, of those years between '60 and '67, the Rat Pack's hey days.

Stories I could—and relive—still tell, once I had some rest.

Upcoming New Release

LOVE ME OR KILL ME
A RAT PACK MYSTERY
BOOK 14
BY
ROBERT J. RANDISI

Vic Damone was known as "The Little Italian" because Dino was "The Big Italian." Vic comes to Eddie to tell him that a fanatic fan of his is threatening to kill Dino so that Vic becomes "The Big Italian."

**For more information
visit: www.SpeakingVolumes.us**